DIRTY STEAL

A DIRTY PLAYERS NOVELLA

DIRTY PLAYERS

LAUREN BLAKELY
KD CASEY

NOTHING TO LOSE PRODUCTIONS

Copyright © 2022 by Lauren Blakely and KD Casey

Cover Design by KP Simmon

All rights reserved. Without limiting the rights under copyright reserved above, no part of this publication may be reproduced, stored in or introduced into a retrieval system, or transmitted, in any form, or by any means (electronic, mechanical, photocopying, recording, or otherwise) without the prior written permission of both the copyright owner and the above publisher of this book. This contemporary romance is a work of fiction. Names, characters, places, brands, media, and incidents are either the product of the author's imagination or are used fictitiously. The author acknowledges the trademarked status and trademark owners of various products referenced in this work of fiction, which have been used without permission. The publication/use of these trademarks is not authorized, associated with, or sponsored by the trademark owners. This book is licensed for your personal use only. This book may not be re-sold or given away to other people. If you would like to share this book with another person, please purchase an additional copy for each person you share it with, especially if you enjoy sexy romance novels with alpha males. If you are reading this book and did not purchase it, or it was not purchased for your use only, then you should return it and purchase your own copy. Thank you for respecting the author's work.

ALSO BY

Also by KD Casey

Unwritten Rules Series

Unwritten Rules

Fire Season

Diamond Ring

Standalone

One True Outcome

Also by Lauren Blakely

Big Rock Series

Big Rock

Mister O

Well Hung

Full Package

Joy Ride

Hard Wood

Happy Endings Series

Come Again

Shut Up and Kiss Me

Kismet

My Single-Versary

Ballers And Babes

Most Valuable Playboy

Most Likely to Score

A Wild Card Kiss

Two A Day

Plays Well With Others

Rules of Love Series

The Virgin Rule Book

The Virgin Game Plan

The Virgin Replay

The Virgin Scorecard

Hopelessly Bromantic Duet (MM)

Hopelessly Bromantic

Here Comes My Man

Men of Summer Series (MM)

Scoring With Him

Winning With Him

All In With Him

The Guys Who Got Away Series

Dear Sexy Ex-Boyfriend

The What If Guy

Thanks for Last Night

The Dream Guy Next Door

The Gift Series

The Engagement Gift

The Virgin Gift

The Decadent Gift

The Extravagant Series

One Night Only

One Exquisite Touch

My One-Week Husband

MM Standalone Novels

A Guy Walks Into My Bar

One Time Only

The Bromance Zone

The Best Men (Co-written with Sarina Bowen)

The Heartbreakers Series

Once Upon a Real Good Time

Once Upon a Sure Thing

Once Upon a Wild Fling

Boyfriend Material

Asking For a Friend

Sex and Other Shiny Objects

One Night Stand-In

Lucky In Love Series

Best Laid Plans

The Feel Good Factor

Nobody Does It Better

Unzipped

Always Satisfied Series

Satisfaction Guaranteed

Instant Gratification

Overnight Service

Never Have I Ever

PS It's Always Been You

Special Delivery

The Sexy Suit Series

Lucky Suit

Birthday Suit

From Paris With Love

Wanderlust

Part-Time Lover

One Love Series

The Sexy One

The Only One

The Hot One

The Knocked Up Plan

Come As You Are

Standalones

Stud Finder

The V Card

The Real Deal

Unbreak My Heart

The Break-Up Album

The Caught Up in Love Series

The Pretending Plot

The Dating Proposal

The Second Chance Plan

The Private Rehearsal

Seductive Nights Series

Night After Night

After This Night

One More Night

A Wildly Seductive Night

ABOUT

One bed, two players, and another chance in this steamy standalone sports romance...

After how this season has gone so far — don't ask — the last thing I need is a distraction.

Like, say, my spring training one-night stand showing up in my dugout. If it's not annoying enough that the hot new shortstop with the heart-stopping smile has been traded to my team, the golden guy now needs a place to stay.

When one of my big-mouthed teammates suggests the new star player shack up in my spare room, I've got myself a helluva problem — and it's getting bigger with my eager, interested, and too-sexy teammate sharing my kitchen, my shower...and then, late one night, my bed.

But before I know it, all these late nights together are making me want things I just can't have with my teammate.

And if I'm not careful, he'll be stealing my heart too...

A scorching hot, only-one-bed-in-the-room/teammates-to-lovers, second chance stand-alone romance...

DIRTY STEAL

Want to be the first to learn of sales, new releases, preorders and special freebies from Lauren Blakely and KD Casey? Sign up for the MM VIP mailing list here!

1

Derek Miller

Here's the thing about fundraisers: After the first flute of champagne, the first circuit of the room, they're kinda uneventful. Worse, you're stuck in your finest suit, in Arizona, in a bar filled with all the guys you saw a few hours ago at the ballpark, who are equally uncomfortable in their suits.

Sure, this is for a good cause. I mean, who doesn't love rescue dogs? The Little Friends charity asked me for a testimonial beforehand to use for its marketing. Major leaguers and our beloved animals. I told them about Ultimate, our dog growing up. She was the ultimate mutt, and I used to hide under the covers with her if there was a big storm. Well, I didn't share the second part. Doesn't match the big league image.

An hour in, the fundraiser isn't so bad. It's spring training, so at least I get to admire-slash-casually ogle my teammates and rivals all stuffed into suits that probably fit their leaned-down October bodies better. Definitely worse ways to pass the time than semi-covert visual appreciation of other players while sipping mid-priced champagne. Eventually, though, that turns a little dull.

For whatever reason—maybe to get us in suits, maybe because baseball players without a structured activity tend to get into trouble—this is a casino-themed fundraiser. A bunch of my teammates from the Seattle Pilots cluster around the simulated craps table while the slightly flustered dealer tries to explain to us that no, we can't really bet, and yes, we need to use the fake cash "Bark Bucks" that the charity provided instead.

Predictably, guys are being slightly drunken jerks. The dealer—who has thin dyed-red hair and thinning patience—tries to separate the real money from the fake, while the tip jar next to her goes conspicuously empty.

I muscle my way past a couple of my

teammates—Travis, our first baseman, and Bautista, our third basemen. "Cut it out, assholes." Because as our shortstop, I'm the captain of the infield and they should—probably—listen to me. Also? Just fucking tip.

Bautista snorts. "We're just messing around."

"Time and place," I say.

Except Travis throws another twenty, clearly to be a jerk, because he's both my best friend on the team and a jerk about half the time. *What's the difference between a clubhouse leader and a babysitter?* I reach for the bill, trying to marshal it into the jar, when the fucker actually taps my hand. And look, I might have a reputation for having a quick temper on the field, but that's *on the field*. I'm not going to get into it with a teammate at a casino-themed *dog* fundraiser.

Settle down, Derek. It's just Bark Bucks.

"Any other rules for us, Miller?" Travis bites out.

I guess we are making a little bit of a scene. Terrific. That's what I need as a headline. *Scuffle! At the Charity Event.* Because the next thing I hear is a rumbly voice saying, "I got it."

When I look over, Adam Chason has come around to my side of the table. Just when I thought the night couldn't get worse, the shortstop for the St. Louis Arches—and his too-perfect smile—appears.

The thing about pro ball is that everyone knows everyone else's business. A guy who's all wholesome commercial smile like him? Yeah, we know what *that guy* gets up to when the cameras stop rolling.

All the trouble in the world.

Except Chason doesn't. He's the guy next door. The one who sweeps up the confetti after team celebrations so the clubhouse workers don't have to. That's not my type.

Then again, my type is mostly: hot, available, and down to bang.

You'd think being a major league player would mean being, well, a *major league player*, but all the clichés about the loneliness of the road turned out to be true. At least for me.

In person, Chason is all of the above, emphasis on *hot*. About my height—so six feet and not lying about it like half the players in the league—with dark brown hair, a scrape of artfully maintained stubble. Among spring training-thick ballplayers, he's particularly lean. Strong. *Flexible*. A word I probably shouldn't be thinking as emphatically as I am.

Too bad he's not available. Or he probably isn't, though his finger doesn't have the glint of a ring. It doesn't matter. Doubt he's down to bang.

He's apparently here to make everyone play nice, since he makes two neat piles—the fake and the real money—then leaves the latter on the table.

"Here you go." He turns to Bautista and Travis. "That wasn't so hard, was it?"

Bautista grumbles something that sounds a lot like *hall monitor*. Travis scoffs, then adds a one-dollar bill.

"Generous," Chason deadpans. He pulls out his wallet, withdraws a fifty, then stuffs it in the jar. Then, he turns to me. Shrugs. Smiles. Travis and Bautista roll their eyes and leave.

"Sorry," Chason says, once they're gone. "Didn't mean to step on your toes."

"Better they're pissed off at you than me."

"True. Some guys forget they're not in a clubhouse…" He trails off, shaking his head.

The pile of real money is still sitting on the table. I scoop it up and stuff it in the jar. "Thanks, man."

A slight grin. A glimpse of even white teeth. Chason taps the pile of fake money with a knuckle. He's quiet, like he's working through something. Like why he came over here. Though his broadening smile might hint at his real reason.

I'm usually pretty good at reading people. I have to be to spot the tilt of a base runner's shoulders before he takes off. To navigate all the personalities in a clubhouse. To sense an argument before it happens like an oncoming storm.

Or in this case, hearing an...undercurrent.

So I ask, "You want in?"

2

Adam Chason

Things I just learned about fundraisers: if you show up to one without your girlfriend, because she's now your ex-girlfriend, people invariably ask where she is.

Even though it's the first week of spring training. Even though she lives in Houston. But a year ago, she was here with me. At this event. So now, I've been fending off questions about Talia all night.

So fun.

What happened? A story in three parts: We were together. Then we weren't. Then I had to leave for spring training. What did it? A great question. Not one I want to answer while surrounded by a bunch of ballplayers sweating in suits. So I've been shrugging it off.

As fundraisers go, this one is fine. I was hoping there'd be dogs here, because one of the best ways to conceal that I'm shy at parties is to find and pet the nearest dog. Dogs don't want anything from you other than some attention; you can't say the wrong thing to a dog as long as you're scratching between its ears.

People, though—people are more complicated. Which is why I busied myself with a glass of champagne, a quick rotation, patting a few guys in greeting, returning to the same script most people use when reuniting at spring training. *Wow, man, looking thick.*

Now, here I am, about to put fake money down at craps, standing next to Derek. In my five years in the league, I've always thought he was good-looking, but, distantly, like a celebrity. Mostly, he is one—an almost-superstar on a team that's defied everyone's expectations.

It's easy to forget about my relationship woes as Derek gives me a slow once-over that starts with my shoes and works its way upward. Which, damn. It's been a while since anyone's looked at me *like that*. (My recent relationship? Let's not talk about that. This is a night for two D things: dogs and denial. If Derek keeps looking at me like that, maybe three D things.)

His hungry stare is about as subtle as a thunderstorm; it sends sparks down the back of my neck. It's been a long time. Too long.

So I check him out right back.

It's not exactly a hardship. The man looks...good. Really good. Perfectly messed up dirty blond hair, bright blue eyes, a suit that looks like he poured himself into it, rippling slightly in the shoulders. With that attitude, a slight aloof edge like he's too cool to be having a conversation with me. Which he probably is.

Except, he just asked me a question.

One my brain stalled on, but now restarts. I repeat it: "Do I want in?"

A slight eye roll. "Yes, Chason"—he says my name the way most people do, like *chasing*, but dropping the *g* and not *Haz-on* with an *H* that starts in your throat—"you want in? It's a game. You bet money."

That snaps me out of my ogling, which might have gone on too long. I recover quickly. "You mean Bark Bucks?"

He holds up a wad of them. "Sounds like you're just scared to lose."

A challenge said teasingly. Though, players compete over everything—batting stats, bubble gum-blowing contests, apparently Bark Bucks. "Well, then I'll have to get in."

"Let's do it," he says with a glint in his eyes.

For the first time all night I'm okay without having a dog to talk to.

So we play. Or try to. Because neither of us *actually* knows the rules. The croupier, whose name tag reads "Deb," attempts the impossible task of explaining things to half-listening, half-drunk ballplayers, who might play a sport with a lot of intricacies but who aren't necessarily great at absorbing those rules.

Like, er, me.

Deb explains how craps works. Twice. But something—the champagne, the press of guys in a relatively small space, how Derek's shoulder brushes against mine—prevents me from listening to what she's saying.

"It'd probably be easier to just play," Derek says, though he sounds more amused than irritated. Or it's possible he's laughing at the carpeted table surface that says "Come" in large letters.

I wave to him, unwilling to admit I don't know what I'm doing. "You first."

He plunks down a few chips, a wad of bright pink Bark Buck bills, then takes the dice Deb gives him. He holds them out, displaying them like he's expecting me to do something. Is craps the one where people blow on the dice? It must be, because he nods like he's daring me to do it.

Instead I tap my hand against his, then knock back a gulp of champagne. Even though it's warmed, it tastes pretty good. That fizzing feeling lasts through Derek casting his dice then looking to Deb for confirmation.

"Did I do that right?" he asks.

She gives him a warm smile. "You did."

"Thought you knew how to play," I say. It comes out flirtatious. Possibly because I'm flirting with him. The harmless kind that won't go anywhere. He might not even pick up on it.

But he arches a challenging eyebrow. "You wanna show me how it's done?"

Or maybe he will pick up on it.

I know nothing about craps. But flirting is all instinct and the next words out of my mouth are, "If you ask nicely."

Derek's lips curve. "Maybe that's not my style," he says.

What is your style? I'd like to ask. Instead, I keep it subtle. "So you're not nice?" I ask.

Derek blinks. I've surprised him. Hell, I've surprised myself.

Even though the table has mostly cleared out, we're still standing close. I should move, interject some space between us, for about a hundred reasons.

Starting with we're both ballplayers. On opposing teams. Well, they would be opposing if my team was any good, which is another issue.

Another issue is—I'm supposed to be upstanding. *Nice.* Or so my parents keep reminding me. But maybe I'm not so nice, since I get a few flashes of what Derek might look like sprawled out on the plain white sheets of my beige little rental house bed.

He rolls.

A three and a one.

I picture his lips parted as I move down his chest.

A four and a six.

I hear the sounds he makes as I travel closer.

A two and a three.

I feel the urgency in his body.

Oh, that's five, and Derek practically crows the way he might after hitting a home run, arms psyched with victory. At some point, he takes off his suit jacket; the fabric of his shirt is thin. My reminder to myself not to check him out diminishes like a glass of champagne.

He gathers the dice, slapping them into my hand. "Your turn, Chason." A smirk. "Unless you want me to blow on them."

"Yes, Miller, please blow on them," I counter, getting into this rhythm faster than I expected. I hold out my hand, dice displayed for his approval, and receive a puff of air across my palm. It shouldn't—*shouldn't* being the operative word—do it for me. But, fuck, it does.

"There," he says." That's your luck."

Luck. I like the sound of that. "Let's see if I'm lucky." I throw, squinting to see what numbers are displayed. A combination adding up to six. "Is that good or bad?"

With that, Derek laughs. "You tell me."

3

Derek

After one glass of champagne, Adam Chason is handsome, put together, and apparently kind of shy. *Adam.* He feels like an Adam now to me. Attraction will do that to a guy. After a few more glasses, Adam loosens the top button of his collar, rolls his shirt up his forearms, and laughs, big, easy, like all that shyness got shed with his suit jacket.

If that's what taking the jacket off does, what about the rest of his clothes? I admit, I'm curious. I could use a helluva distraction for one night, especially considering the shitty start to spring training so far. Yeah, it's spring training but I don't like to underperform ever, and the last few days haven't been my best. Blowing off steam is always good for a reset on the diamond. I didn't have *Flirt with the league's golden boy* on my bingo card for the evening—and I definitely didn't have him flirting right back.

But this twist works for me.

Except the evening is wrapping up, the bar subtly then not so subtly turning up its lights to encourage us all to split. Spring training mornings start early. I *should* go home and get some sleep. Adam isn't leaving either, casually leaning against the high lip of the table, displaying the toned muscles of his forearms. Maybe he's lingering because, like me, he's got nothing at home but an empty bed.

Maybe he'll take me up on an offer to fill it.

The lights come up, the bar switching from *subtle* to *GTFO*, players giving each other thumped-hug goodbyes. Some are sauntering over to the main area, now filling with patrons, to continue the party, seemingly unbothered by the fact that this is a gay bar. I could stay, flirt, pick up, find someone who's obvious in his interests. Whose flicked looks over at me might be a little more calculated than Adam's.

Or I could stay right here. I've always loved a challenge. Especially when I need one. And I definitely need one.

It'd be easier if Adam wasn't getting his jacket, rolling down his sleeves, literally buttoning his wholesome self back up. "You heading home?" he asks.

"Depends, I guess."

He raises a dark eyebrow. "On?"

"On if the party's staying here too." I might overemphasize *party*, but subtlety sometimes doesn't get you laid.

But Adam's quiet, looking almost spooked. Ah, fuck. Don't need to be coming on too strong. Or, honestly, at all. I've never hooked up with a ballplayer before. But it's not like I have a great track record with non-ballplayers either. "I shouldn't..." he trails off.

An unfinished statement laced with none of his previous flirtation.

Un-subtlety doesn't get me laid either. I swallow my disappointment with a gulp of champagne, then toss a goodbye at the room as I walk out to call myself an Uber.

Or would. A hundred other guys all have the same idea, and the app flashes a message: ***Looking for a driver in your area.*** Great. Thanks, app.

I slouch—it's not sulking if I do it on

purpose—against the stuccoed exterior wall of the bar, refresh my app, and wait. And wait. And…

An Uber pings. Uber Pool. Normally I'm okay with it. There are worse things than riding in awkward silence with a few strangers. Though maybe not with Adam's rejection still stinging.

But fine, if that's my only option, I'll take it. I hit accept and am granted a magical two-minute wait time. An Uber pulls up, a compact sedan with a bunch of boxes piled up in the front seat. I guess I'm squeezing in the back. This night keeps getting better.

Especially after I confirm my name with the driver as yes, *that* Derek M.

"Cool. I've got another pickup right here," he says.

Who climbs in a second later, apologizing for having made the driver wait all of three minutes, but Adam fucking Chason?

"Oh, hey," he says awkwardly.

"Hey," I mutter, but I hope that's the last of it. The driver doesn't move for a second. Is there going to be a third big leaguer squeezed in with us in this tiny backseat? But then he puts the car in gear, pulling out into the Phoenix night. The car seems even smaller with us in motion, Adam's knee occasionally brushing mine.

"Sorry," Adam says, like he has somewhere else to put his knees, or like I'm going to be mad for him getting cooties on me. I'm mostly mad he *isn't* getting cooties on me. I deliberately brush my knee against his to evoke another half-whispered *sorry* from him.

It's possible I do it again after that. Adam's hands tense on his knees, a tension that matches the one in the car. I shift my legs, again, enjoying the brush of fabric, and the slight color in his cheeks visible in the dimmed backseat lighting. After a second, he shifts too, not like he's uncomfortable with the whole situation but like his pants are suddenly tighter for some reason.

"So, that was...fun," Adam says.

His hesitation is intriguing. Hell, a lot about him is intriguing, a puzzle that doesn't quite fit the image he projects. "Yeah, it wasn't too bad," I say, checking the street signs to see how far away we are.

While I'm looking out the window, there's another swoosh of fabric. This time, he initiated it. Huh. What's his deal? It's not like Mister Shy engineered an Uber pool, but it sure seems like he's trying to engineer something else.

Maybe his *I shouldn't* was supposed to end with *I shouldn't, but...* Because you don't get to be where we are as players without going after what we want. Still, I have questions: If he's not straight and just a little less vocal about it than I am. If this is his first time with another player. He certainly doesn't hesitate in how he drags his knee across mine, even as he's studying the passing houses through the car window.

Maybe his *I shouldn't* was supposed to end with *I shouldn't ask myself over, but I'm going to anyway.*

Do I want to try again with him? Maybe I pegged him all wrong. Maybe he's not the boy next door after all. Before I decide, the driver announces our first destination: my boring rental house that looks like all the others around it. At least I opted to spend spring training alone. If nothing comes of this thing with Adam, I won't have any witnesses to my eventual slightly sad faceplant onto the couch—unlike the regular season where I live in a Seattle high-rise. Down the hall from Travis. Who invites himself over. A lot. I don't mind that much, until he has to witness my inevitable relationship disappointments.

I get out of the car. To my surprise, Adam follows. "My place is a few blocks away. Seemed silly to have him make two stops." He shrugs, like it's obvious, even if most big leaguers generally treat drivers like an automated part of the car. "Which house is yours?"

I have to squint for a second to make out the numbers: a line of them, identical as if they came off a manufacturing line, with identical SUVs out front. "I think it's that one."

"My first night here, I tried my key in the wrong house," Adam says, a little sheepishly.

"No one there to let you in?"

He shakes his head. "Nope." He swallows, meets my gaze straight on. Then, like it takes some serious guts to say this, he adds, "There's no one."

With that, I'm suddenly a whole lot more intrigued.

It seems like he wants to say more—his hands are balled in his pockets, his shoulders curled in slightly. Different from the guy who just nudged my leg in the car. "I just got out of a long-term relationship." Though it sounds more like, *I just got my heart broken.*

"She and I were pretty serious..." He digs a toe into the concrete of the sidewalk.

Which might mean he's down to experiment—I don't mind, exactly, but I need to know what I'm working with here. "Have all your exes been women?" I ask. There. Blunt, even if he doesn't look surprised.

He shakes his head again. "No." A slight smile with that. "I've got a few ex-boyfriends who'd probably also agree that I, quote, *let baseball run my life too much.*"

Something I've heard from everyone I've ever dated—that baseball was my spouse and they were just my hookups. Because it's hard to understand the demands of the season, or that when I say I'll be on the road for half of it, I mean it. With that, the accusation I'm screwing around behind their backs, even though in recent years it's been the opposite. Better to go into this with clear expectations. "Yeah, I feel that."

A broader smile, one subtly different from the familiar Adam Chason commercial-and-endorsements grin, like it's meant just for me, even if I'm offering myself up as a rebound. No fuss, no emotions, just two guys getting what they want and moving on. I ignore the voice in the back of my head that sounds strangely like *What if it could be more than that?* and say, "You wanna come in for a drink?"

"I probably shouldn't drink. Early morning." Though he doesn't start walking in whatever direction his rental house is either.

"The drink was a euphemism, Chason."

"I—Oh." He looks surprised. A touch excited too. "Are you sure?"

"Do you think I don't know what a euphemism is?"

He laughs. "Maybe I don't know what it means."

An invitation, one I take, stepping toward him. Maybe he needs someone to take the lead. Fine by me. He looks even better up close, the Phoenix night darkening his dark hair and eyes. We probably shouldn't kiss, standing on the narrow sidewalk, in full view of other major leaguers likely snooping from the windows of their rental houses. But *probably shouldn't* doesn't mean much given how he's looking at me and wetting his lips with his tongue.

"So about that drink," I say.

"Yeah"—his voice is gratifyingly hoarse—"let's go."

4

Adam

We might as well teleport up the walkway from the sidewalk to the porch. The next thing I know, we're shoving each other into his front hallway. Derek's jacket lands...somewhere, followed by my own. He kisses me—hard, hands at my face, stubble catching the edge of my lips. Whatever euphemism there was is lost in the thrust of his tongue in my mouth.

It doesn't feel particularly nice. Rough in a way that's better for it. A bad idea all around—a one-night stand with a fellow ballplayer, even if we're unlikely to see each other in the regular season—but fuck it. *Fuck it.* Or well, maybe not *it.*

Derek kisses me against the sparsely decorated wall next to his front door. Again in the living room. Again in the short hallway leading back to his bedroom. He makes casual work of my shirt, buttons impatiently undone then one or two sent skidding. I feel similarly unloosed. My belt comes unbuckled, my pants kicked off. Derek squeezes my ass appreciatively, before performing a close and thorough inspection of my chest and stomach, then pressing a slightly nicer kiss than I'm expecting at my waistband, followed by the scrape of teeth.

"Let me blow you," Derek says, like that's some kind of hardship.

I nod, maybe a little frantically, and Derek sinks to his knees then takes me in his mouth, fast, messy, distinctly un-*nice*. I thread my hand in his hair. The strands are tacky from product and residual humidity from being in a crowded bar. I pull his hair and get an affirmative grunt from his busy mouth. He strokes himself through his opened suit pants with a similar impatience, like he's too turned on to wait.

"I can do that for you," I offer, panting, because he's clearly as desperate as I am.

Since he keeps palming himself as he sucks me.

My hips move on their own. I'm forming an apology for thrusting too deep when he pulls off to mutter, "Do that again." His voice already sounds ragged, hot, the way he's hot on his knees, lips red, hair a mess, looking at me like he's been thinking about this all night. Simple, in a way things haven't been in a long time.

Eventually, he pulls off, a flourish and a pop, a wipe of his hand across his mouth. His shirt's still on, more or less, open to reveal the top of his chest, the artwork of his tattoos. Somehow that's sexier than if he was completely naked. I grab myself, a move he eyes with some amusement, then rocks back on his heels. "Impatient?" he asks.

It'd be rude to tell him to get back to it, even if it seems like he wants me to. Possibly for me to beg. "You're good at that," I say.

I'm rewarded with the slow spread of his smile. But no other reaction.

"Could you...?" I ask.

Another smirk. "Could I what?" His question is too innocent. He wants me to ask for it.

I can feel myself flush, which is stupid. I've spent most of my adult life in clubhouses, for fuck's sake. I've heard a lot worse. Hell, in the right mood, I've said a lot worse. But he seems very into getting to debauch *Adam Chason, certified nice guy*, so if that's what he's after, I can at least provide that. "Um"—I put a little uncertainty in my voice—"get back to it?"

"Just wanted to hear you say *suck me off*," Derek says then laughs at me, not entirely nicely.

Fine. I'll play his game. I want the same thing. "Suck me off," I whisper, sounding needy, feeling needier.

"Ah, I knew nice wasn't your style," he says with an appreciative groan. Then takes me back in his mouth. This time, there's no messing around. My cock nudges the back of his throat. He swallows convulsively, enough for me to feel it, and that's it, I'm tipping over the edge, hand in his hair to keep him still as I come.

After, he coughs a few times. "You could warn a guy, Chason."

"It's, uh, Chason." I pronounce it phonetically. "You kinda have to say the *h* in your throat."

"Oh, *sorry*. I had something else in my throat."

"Which you already swallowed," I say drily.

His blue eyes say *well played.* "You sure got a lot of opinions about my throat."

"It's a good throat," I say, and he laughs.

Derek is still on his knees. I offer him a hand up. For a second, we stand there, Derek's mouth a tempting red. I want to kiss him, so I do, a slower kiss than the ones that led us in here, a kiss that doesn't feel like a one-night stand even if that's all this is. Because he's clearly not looking for anything serious. Even if he was, I'm not ready for it. But I'm not going to admit that to a dude I hung out with for the first time tonight, even one whose mouth I just came in.

Talking doesn't seem to be on the agenda for him either. We kiss as we move to his bed, Derek lying back and pulling me down on top of him. His shirt's still on, buttons digging into my chest, and he sits up enough to let me push it off his shoulders. His pants go next, kicked off, leaving him in boxer briefs, giving me a full view of the ink across his chest—a sunburst, dark against his tanned skin. Below that, another tattoo, a constellation of stars descends below the waistband of his briefs.

"You're really hot," I say. *Smooth, Chason. Very deeply smooth.*

At least Derek laughs. We make out for a while, his cock nudging my hip through the fabric of his briefs, even though he doesn't seem like he's in a hurry now. I peel down his last layer of clothes, pausing as he lifts his hips, and reach for his cock, rewarded with a moan against my lips that extends as I stroke him.

We're pressed close, chest to chest, and it feels closer than we should be if this is a one-time thing. If this is nothing more than two guys blowing, pun intended, off some steam together. He kisses my neck, teeth catching like he might leave marks, and that'll be something—walking into the clubhouse with those as a souvenir.

His breathing picks up, especially when I spit in my hand and reapply myself, thumb teasing the edge of his foreskin. "I'm close," he breathes.

"Appreciate the warning."

"Just trying to be polite." He laughs slightly, then groans, deeply, and comes all over my hand.

We lie there for a minute. I try not to wipe my fingers against his bedspread. Possibly sensing my discomfort, he hands me a wad of tissues, then tells me the bathroom is just down the hall. A dismissal, though not a surprising one. There's no point in me lingering, I tell myself. This was only a one-night stand, a way to get Talia worked out of my system. Sticking around would make a weird night even weirder.

When I return to the bedroom, Derek has his boxer briefs pulled back on.

He's lounging against his headboard, scrolling through his phone. "I was gonna get something to eat," he says. His eyes meet mine in a hopeful question. Is he asking me if I want to join? Or is that my cue to leave?

I'm so rusty when it comes to the rules of hookups. I kinda want to stay, but the words that come out are, "I was about to head out."

Since that's easier. *I think.*

"This place does pretty good tacos. Your loss," he says, a little sarcastic but also somewhat let down.

Or maybe I'm imagining his look of slight disappointment before he schools his face back into the challenging, *I dare you to strike me out* expression I know from game broadcasts.

"Thanks though," I add. "I just got out of a relationship and..."

Ugh. The stuff with Talia is too much to explain. It all still feels too private, too fresh. Really, does he even want to hear it?

"It's all good, Chason," he says, deliberately overemphasizing my name this time.

"Ah, you're a fast learner," I remark as I pick up my clothes, trying to futilely unwrinkle them, even if the only witnesses to my walk of not-quite-shame will be whatever desert critters are brave enough to crawl out into the road.

"I am," he says, then takes a beat, his eyes traveling up and down me again. "So are you. At least when you're impatient and really want something."

My face burns. Pretty sure if we didn't work in the same small world, I might ask him if he's free tomorrow night. If I can return the favor on my knees.

Hell, with his tacos comment, maybe he was about to do the same.

But once is for the best.

I need to focus on baseball and finding a way to win. Even if that's not likely for my team this season.

Once I'm dressed, Derek walks me to the door, still clad only in his boxer briefs. He looks sleepy, hair in disarray. Adorable, really. It makes me want to stay, even if I know I shouldn't press my luck. Derek gets the door, unlatching it, opening it so that he won't be visible to the street.

"Enjoy the tacos," I say.

He gives a small smile. "Enjoy spring training."

Then, impulsively, I grab his face and press a hot, fast goodbye kiss to his lips.

When I break apart, he looks unsteady, whispers, *whoa*.

A small dose of pride spreads in me. I knocked him off kilter, like he did to me tonight. "By the way, is five your lucky number?"

With that, a *you remembered* smile. "I think it was. Night, Chason."

And I'm dispensed out onto the porch. The door closes. For a second, I consider raising my hand, knocking to be let back in. But no, that's not how this works. So I pull out my phone and enter the address of my rental house. At least I can cleanly navigate my way home.

* * *

For the rest of spring training, I only see Derek once. The Arches play the Pilots at their park, and we both start. I reach first on an error then advance to third base on a single, flying past him at short.

Mostly, I'm thinking about scoring.

But partly I'm wondering what I'll say if I

run into him later. In the corridor. Outside the park. *Want tacos? How's your spring training? Have you learned how to play craps yet?*

Why am I even practicing opening lines?

That's a good question.

One I don't find the answer to as I field my position in the next inning. As I watch Derek work a walk. As I wonder what it would be like to tag him out on the next play.

The batter at the plate hits a weak grounder to our second baseman, who's set up in the shallow outfield. He flips the ball to me as I hurry to cover second; I drop my foot on the bag as Derek hustles down the basepath, then throw onto first for a bang-bang double play that ends the inning.

My teammates begin their retreat to the dugout, but Derek is still there, uniform streaked with dirt like he can't believe I turned two on him. Huh. I've never played against a guy I hooked up with. It's kind of awesome. A little like having a delicious secret.

Especially when Derek shakes his head and says, "You sure you got your foot on the bag?"

Like I faked out tagging second base. "I'm sure. If you want, I could tag you out again."

I'm not trying to flirt with him, but it

comes out that way, even if it probably just sounds like regular, harmless trash talk to my teammates. That may be all Derek hears too.

"Now there's a thought," he says.

So maybe he heard me correctly. I lift the glove to my face to hide a smile, but then seize the chance and add, "A good thought."

He lifts a brow, then his lips curve into a dirty grin. "You have so many good ideas."

"I do." I'm *this* close to jumping on the chance he's maybe offering, to asking if he wants to meet again. But is this just harmless flirting? Or the start of something more that I'm not ready for yet?

I stall too long. Before I know it, Derek is heading off the field with a tip of his cap.

After the game, we load up on the team bus. I look back one more time. My pulse kicks faster when I see him in the distance, leaving the facility.

Maybe I've found my answer to the *Why did I want to run into him?* question. That one night with Derek last month was both challenging and easy at the same time.

I think I like that combo.

But I turn my gaze away and focus on baseball. That's what I do for the rest of spring training and into the first few months of the season.

I play hard, and I go home alone. Sometimes, before I fall asleep, I check his game stats to see how his spring is going.

Mostly, he's playing well enough.

Mostly.

5

Adam

On a Monday night in late June, the mood is dreary.

I cross home plate in the bottom of the eighth, having just knocked in two runs. Ordinarily, I'd high five some teammates. Batting runs in is, obviously, one of the most satisfying parts of playing baseball for a living. It'd be more satisfying if the Arches scored more than the other team.

Since we're trailing by five, no one comes out of the dugout. It's just another night in St. Louis, like most of the ones this season.

When the game ends the way most games this season have ended, no one in the clubhouse says *Want to grab a bite?* or *Better luck tomorrow.*

But the mood shifts Tuesday morning when I arrive at the clubhouse for an early workout.

The second I push open the door, the vibe among my teammates is...curious.

Chatty.

My skin tingles.

I know this vibe. My teammates are clustered toward one end of the stalls, whispering loudly. There's pretty much one reason they'd be doing that.

A trade.

I feel a burst of anticipation that surprises me, then a little too much hope.

One of my teammates says my name—"Chason" with a full *ch*. I clear my throat to alert them to my presence. Conversation stops. Our center fielder turns slowly, chair squeaking. "I think they need to talk with you."

They could mean anyone: our manager, the team's president of baseball operations, my agent. I leave the changing area. When I reach our manager's office, my agent is waiting for me outside. He's also become a good friend over the years.

I figured I'd see Maddox LeGrande today

—he told me he was coming to town. The fact that he's here now means only one thing, and it's not that we're having lunch. "Hey, Adam," he says, since he's one of the few people who uses my first name. The sliver of a smile says the rest. The news is good. As in…I'm going somewhere that wins. "Wanted to be the first to tell you."

"Trade?" I ask, though the question is a formality. I've been playing well this season and the rest of the team…hasn't. Something increasingly difficult to talk around during press scrums. Maddox nods, looking pleased. "How's Seattle sound to you?"

Holy shit. That takes a few seconds to sink in. *Seattle.* "Are you sure?" Like there's been some mistake. Because Seattle already has a shortstop, who's an accomplished hitter. Defender. *Kisser.* My tongue was in his mouth just a few months ago.

"Great," I say, like that one word can mask how I feel—a little guilty, like I shouldn't be this excited to go to a club with a winning record, and a lot weird.

Because, well, it wasn't just my tongue in Derek's mouth. But I swipe dirty thoughts from my brain, as Maddox ushers me into the manager's office, even as something else nags at me. Something I'll deal with later.

I must look as bewildered as I feel, because my manager starts talking about all the great times I've had in St. Louis, about how much there is left to accomplish in my career. About how change is *hard*—baseball's motto for when something difficult happens to someone else.

His speech ends with an offered hand. I shake, then get pulled in for a hug. I knew a trade was coming. Even though it's good—hell it's great—it's still hard, something that sets in as I say goodbye to my teammates, the team personnel, and the ballpark staff. As I pack up what I'll need from my apartment and arrange to have the rest of my things shipped. As I get on a chartered flight to Seattle, wondering what's going to happen.

That's what's nagging at me—the Seattle Pilots don't need two shortstops. Either they're floating the idea of trading Derek—doubtful, even if he's had a slightly slow start to the year—or one of us will have to play a different position.

And that's the other problem. *Positions*. A slightly hysterical thought. Because I can imagine him in a lot of positions, none of which have to do with baseball. I should let it go. We hooked up and only spoke once on the field. Do guys normally think about their hookups for months after?

I have four hours to think about it on the plane from St. Louis to Seattle, then on the brief drive from the airport to the ballpark. Seattle seems like a cool city, modern and young, though I've no idea of where to start apartment hunting. When I scroll through listings, everything already has double-digit offers and bids.

Maybe someone on the team will have suggestions. Too bad there's no one to turn to and ask a thornier question. *Hey, how do I face my spring training hookup again when I see him in the same clubhouse in, oh, say, thirty fucking minutes?*

I drop my face in my hands.

I'm good at baseball. But there's no handbook for awkward post blow job friendships. Guess I'll just have to figure it out.

* * *

The ballpark sits downtown, its roof domed against the slightly gray sky. A peppy handler meets me at the players' entrance then shepherds me into an office with the team president and Pilots manager.

I do my best to focus, but I'm thinking

about what comes next the whole time. That moment when I walk into the clubhouse feeling like the new kid in class. Man, I wish there were dogs here too.

When I make it to the clubhouse, it's as awkward as I imagined. A few guys murmur greetings. I say hi back. Then my gaze swings to Derek, who's taking off his shirt.

Because of course I walk in right when he's getting undressed. Thanks, universe.

And when I scan the stalls, of course, mine is right next to his.

Someone has a funny sense of humor.

I swallow roughly, wondering where to look. Out of the corner of my eye, I take stock of the guy I hooked up with.

I don't usually do hookups—with men or women.

Derek looks even better—still broad in the shoulders if leaned down from his spring training bulk. I have to admit, I have a thing for tattoos, partly because I don't have any. His ink looks even better in the daylight. Intriguing. I follow its tracery down his torso and want to follow it with my—

...And he's looking right at me, with a scrunched expression, like he's not sure what I'm doing there. Which, same.

For a second, we just look at each other, questions passing between us we can't ask. Like if he's cool with my being here. For one thing, neither of us has much say in the matter. For another, the answer is probably *no*. I also have no idea what I'm supposed to say to any of my new teammates. *Psyched to join you?* Ugh. That's trying too hard for the new guy. *Happy to be here*. Though I'm not sure I am quite yet, even if I'm more likely to get a ring here than in St. Louis.

A question presses against my tongue. *Is he thinking about me like I'm thinking about him?* Or is he just thinking about which of us is going to play at short.

Finally, so I don't stand around like a dingus who's never been in a clubhouse, I step forward, drop my stuff in the stall, and turn to him. Screw the weirdness. I have to deal with my new teammate, whether or not I want to strip off his uniform pants.

"Hey, Derek," I say.

At least he pulls on a shirt. "Hey, Chason. Guess you won't be turning two on me any longer," he says drily, a reference to our last encounter.

Which makes my pulse spike—that he remembers the details.

This is awfully inconvenient. Being

attracted to my teammate. "Let's hope not," I say.

"You enjoying Seattle so far?"

"Yeah, all two hours of it."

"I'm guessing you just found out this morning about the trade?" he asks.

"My agent came by to tell me."

"Gotta love a business where you start work in one town and finish it in another," he says, kind of easygoing, and I do not know what to make of Derek Miller. I'd expect him to freeze me out. But he's sort of...inviting.

It's weird, but kind of cool.

"It's not a bad town to finish the day in," he adds.

Before I can say anything else, a couple other guys on the team swing by, with Travis and Bautista joining in. Are they the kind of guys who carry a grudge? Are we going to relitigate the casino dog fundraiser incident on top of everything else?

I hope not. Bautista extends a hand, shaking mine. "Welcome to Seattle."

"Happy to be here," I manage.

Travis offers a clap on the back hug, which I return. Maybe he can sense my discomfort. "No hard feelings about that dog thing, bro."

There's my answer and it's a welcome relief.

"As long as you play well," Travis adds, with a wink. Got it. As a first baseman, he has two real talents: hitting the ball hard and making small talk with base runners. He seems especially good at the latter, since he keeps going, "Where do they have you staying?"

"At a hotel for now. The team made reservations at a place nearby."

Next to him, Bautista cringes. "Dude. You don't want to stay for long in this neighborhood."

"Why not?"

"It's boring, and full of athletes," he says.

Derek rolls his eyes. "Sounds awful."

"Thanks for the tip," I say. "I was looking at apartment listings on the plane. Guess the market's pretty tight, but I'll make sure to look *not* near here."

Bautista laughs. "Fast learner." Then his eyes flicker, and he nudges Derek in the arm. "Hey, don't you have an extra room since Grady left?"

Oh shit.

Derek's smile tightens. "Yep, sure do," he says, firmly. Like the conversation is over.

No. Just no. Bautista has to stop *now*. My stomach churns.

But he continues on, oblivious. "Hope you have better luck than I did. Took me a while to get a realtor to even take my calls. I mean, I thought, I'm a big leaguer, they gotta be accommodating. But nope. Maybe I should have posed as a tech bro."

"The hotel's fine. I really don't mind," I say quickly. Because I can see where this is going and it's toward Derek's spare room.

"Nah, man, that gets depressing after like a week. I'd offer you a room in my place but it's being renovated," Bautista urges, then turns to Derek, imploring him. "Miller, do the new guy a solid. Let him stay with you till he finds a place."

Derek makes a noise that's a cross between agreement and choking.

This can't happen. I can't slide into town, join the team, then crash at his place. That's the definition of *not cool*. It's also the definition of entirely too tempting. "Seriously, a hotel is fine," I interject.

Travis's meaty paw lands on my shoulder. "You'll like it there." He gives a chin nod to Derek. "What do you say?"

Derek's face goes stony. He clearly doesn't want this, but if I protest again, I'll look like a jackass in front of my new teammates for showing up a veteran player. Derek takes a deep breath. "Sure, Chason"—he says my last name the way it's actually pronounced—"you can crash with me for a while."

I'm at another loss for words, this one not driven by shyness, but by the sheer effing cluster of this situation. "Thanks, man. Appreciate it." Like I'm not taking his fielding position—and now his spare bedroom.

6

Adam

Thinking about staying at Derek's place carries me through the game that night. Since I'm not in the lineup for the game, I park myself at the dugout railing and try to learn as much as I can about my new team. Watching Derek on TV gave me a healthy aesthetic appreciation for his fielding. Watching him like this is completely different.

He's magnetic—in how he moves, an economy of motions as he scoops balls hit into the middle infield and relays them to the other fielders. Until he makes a throwing error in the fifth inning, mishandling a ball that allows the runner to score. An error that could have happened to anyone, but Derek gives our dugout a long look after it, like he's waiting for our manager to pull him.

The Pilots—*we,* though the designation is still strange—win the game. At least that's something different from St. Louis. Inside the clubhouse, I'm at my stall changing out of my uniform when Derek comes over. "I was about to head out, if you're ready," he says.

Travis and Bautista aren't around. It's just us talking. I should give Derek one more chance to back out of the extreme awkwardness of sharing his home with someone he once blew and now works with.

"Thanks again," I say, "But you really don't have to do this." I toss my jersey—damp from the ambient humidity and the effort of standing in a dugout for three hours—into a nearby laundry cart. "I'm sure the hotel is fine."

"It's all good," he reassures me. "Bautista wasn't kidding about the market up here. Besides, I got a spare bed." Though his voice hitches slightly on the word *bed.*

Now I can't decline without looking ungrateful. "Okay. Sure," I say, but my biggest concern isn't actually appearances; it's being in the same space with someone I'm too attracted to.

Derek waits as I change into my street clothes while one of the clubhouse attendants fetches my suitcases from storage. We walk in silence out of the clubhouse, down the long hallway to the players' parking lot.

He pops the hatch of his truck. I load my suitcases, grateful for the momentary respite from awkwardness. *This is only temporary.* Even if being near him is bringing back memories in flashes: The way his knee brushed mine during that short Uber ride. The way he kissed me against his front door. And the way I walked home in a daze after, my lips stinging, wondering if I made a mistake hooking up with him. Wondering if I made a mistake by taking off too soon.

"You all set?" he calls from the front seat. Because of course I've spent a solid minute arranging suitcases. I'm not avoiding him. I just...don't want to have a conversation either.

"Yeah." I close the hatch. *This is temporary. It's just a spare room. Be cool, Chason.* Ha. Like it's that easy.

The drive to South Lake Union on the waterfront is mercifully short. Derek plays tour guide as night falls, pointing out trendy restaurants, music clubs I doubt I'd ever go to, and, of course, too many coffee shops to count. All artisan, naturally. But he's impersonal, like he might be with an out-of-town guest he barely knows. Except he glances over a few times, probably when he thinks I'm not looking.

I'm looking. I'm keenly aware of the space we occupy.

Eventually, we arrive at his condo, in a high-rise overlooking Lake Union. He insists on helping with one of my suitcases, which he parks in the front hallway. The place looks like most big leaguers' condos: clean and slightly sterile, with framed memorabilia on the walls. A dining room that looks barely used and a living room that looks much more lived in, centered on a massive entertainment center. I catch my reflection in the TV screen. At least I'm hiding how weird I think this whole situation is, even if he probably feels the same way.

I look around, hoping to find something to talk about—a family photo maybe. But there's nothing like that except pictures of various teams and tournaments. Derek, with his arms around other players, smiling in victory.

Except—

"Who's this?" I ask, trying not to coo and

failing. Because the picture on his end table is of a kid recognizable as a young Derek with his arms around a fluffy, golden-furred dog.

Derek offers a real smile for the first time since Bautista volunteered a spare room. "Oh, that's Ultimate. She was my dog growing up."

"She looks like a sweetheart."

"Yeah"—his voice goes a little wistful—"she really was."

I pick up the picture, studying the pup. "Mutt? A little golden, a little lab, a little something else?"

Another smile. "Hence the name Ultimate. Ultimate mutt."

"Did you pick her name?"

"I did," he says, chest puffing up.

"That's a good name," I remark as I set down the photo.

"Thanks, Chason. I was hoping you'd approve," he deadpans. Finally, we're back to an easy rhythm. Like the night of the fundraiser.

So I stay there, on that frequency. I *like* this frequency. "It's kind of funny. I was hoping there were going to be dogs at the casino thing. You know, to hang out with," I say. "Since it was for a dog rescue."

"You were hoping to play poker with a dog?"

I laugh. "Sure. If any played. Or just to talk to."

He nods faux-thoughtfully. "So was I better company than a dog?"

I shrug, since I'm not giving in that easily. Besides, he won't want me too. "You're aiming pretty high, Miller."

He rolls his eyes. "Pretty sure I hit the mark."

No doubt. "I mean, sure," I say, like I'm not giving an inch. "I suppose."

"I didn't hear any complaints," he says, maybe fishing for compliments. This is another side of him I'm learning. At the fundraiser, he was all edges and cocksure attitude. Then at his place, he was playful and pushy. Now, he's...*interested*.

Same here, but that's risky. "Fair enough. You worked out okay," I tease.

Derek gestures like he's spinning something with his hand.

I raise my eyebrows in question.

"The picture of Adam Chason is filling in now. You went to the party to talk to a dog, but then you found me."

Come to think of it, that's exactly what I did. I found him at the party, flirted with him, went home with him. Now, here I am again, in his house, sliding right back into the way we were that night. A little teasing, a little pushing.

"You were decent enough company," I joke.

Derek tosses his head back, laughing, like he can't believe I said that. "Why am I letting you stay here?"

Suddenly, I snap back to reality, worried I've gone too far. "I can stay at a hotel if it's a problem."

His hand comes down on my shoulder. "Enough. I wouldn't have agreed if I wasn't cool with it." He motions to my suitcase. "Let me show you your room."

And that's that. With a few words, he's reassured me that I'm not unwelcome. I needed that. *A lot*.

"That'd be great," I say, grabbing my bags. "And thanks again."

"Happy to help," he says, heading down the hall. Then, as he turns, he says over his shoulder, "Since I know you liked my company more than a dog's. Evidently, that's a high compliment from you." He goes into the room before I can respond.

My face flushes. Heat slides down my back from all these reminders of that night together. A night that ended too soon? Maybe it did. But a repeat isn't in the cards now that I'm staying here.

Somehow, I need to erase the memories of that night. It helps that his spare bedroom has all the personality of a hotel. Some art that the decorator must have picked out, a bed, a dresser mounted with a TV. "That's...the bed," he says, gesturing helpfully, as if I can't figure out what the big piece of furniture in the middle of the room is. He swipes a hand over his face like he can't believe he said that either. "You know, that thing you sleep on."

"I'm familiar with beds," I say.

"Yeah, same here," he mutters, his eyes darkening, like maybe he's remembering the last time we were in his bedroom. Together... *Same here*. He quickly heads to the door, then gestures to the en suite. "Bathroom's that way. Feel free to spread out as much as you want."

In a hurry, he leaves me to unpack, which I do as little as possible, feeling very much like an unwanted guest, even though he's definitely tried to welcome me. I hear Derek moving around in the other room, opening and closing cabinets, turning on, then muting the TV.

My new temporary roommate appears in the doorway a minute later. "I was going to make something to eat. Want anything?" At least that's familiar and easier to handle than sleeping arrangements that remind us of sex. Ballplayers' favorite subject: food, and the preparation and consumption thereof. With that, comes the memory that I didn't stick around last time to eat.

Even thinking about a meal, I can't seem to escape that night in spring training.

"Food would be great," I say then follow him into the kitchen.

He parks me on a barstool at his kitchen island, as he starts rummaging through his fridge. I expected either takeout or prepared meals, but it seems like he's actually going to *make me* something.

That's another surprise. I wasn't expecting a cook. "Sandwiches okay?" he asks.

Like I can turn down food on top of a room. "Derek…" I have no idea what to say. Maybe I should call him *Miller*. "You don't have to make me din—" I stop before I act like this is a big deal. He offered sandwiches. The most casual possible food. *Like tacos.* Thanks, brain.

His hands flex on the countertop. "I'm hungry. I bet you are too," he says, glancing at the clock. It's ten. "I have a couple kinds of bread, some turkey, probably some pastrami somewhere."

Great. Now we're talking about sandwich preferences. Wheat or white. Mayo or mustard. Moments ago we were chatting about dogs, the night we met, and *beds*. Fucking beds. Tonight is topsy turvy.

Well, what did you think shacking up with the guy you wanted a repeat with would be like?

There it is. The sharp, clear awareness of my wants. For some reason, maybe it's chemical, maybe it's more, I wanted a repeat.

I still do.

That's the problem.

"Whatever is fine," I say, past the dryness in my mouth.

"Chason—" he begins, and that feels personal, somehow, with the rumble of it in his throat. He's interrupted by a loud pounding on the door. "Fuck. That must be Travis."

Derek strides to the door and yanks it open to reveal Travis, who's holding a six-pack already missing a beer.

Travis salutes me as he comes in with a "'Sup, Chason," then spots the open sleeve of bread, and points. "Ooh, sandwiches. Make me one."

Derek rolls his eyes fondly, then prepares

a sandwich without asking Travis his preferences. When he's done, he turns to me, holding up bread and gesturing vaguely to the layout of condiments and meat.

"You want mayo?" he asks, as if the real question isn't *What the fuck are we all doing?* I'm too shy to ask when we're alone, and Derek's too nonchalant. Except for the tightness to his smile that Travis doesn't seem to notice.

I eye the pack of deli meat next to Derek—pastrami stacked neatly on a piece of waxed paper. "Pastrami with…mayo?" I try, and fail, to hide my skepticism.

Derek's eyebrows scrunch slightly. Now I feel bad. "What do you normally eat pastrami with?"

"Usually with mustard on rye."

He nods like he's absorbing some received wisdom, not a sandwich recipe. "Cheese?"

I shake my head.

"You sure?" Like he's concerned about not being a good host. "I think I have some Swiss somewhere."

"I don't eat meat and cheese together." Another eyebrow scrunch, this one bordering on cute. "I'm Jewish," I clarify. "Assumed it was obvious from the name."

Derek looks briefly surprised. "Is there

other food I should get?" he asks, which is kind of cool, actually, but also implies I'm going to be staying here a while.

And I can't, if the last hour is anything to go by. Not sure I can last this long with my attraction to him.

"I'm good. If I'm still here in a week"—I might combust, semi-spontaneously from being around him all the time—"we can do some shopping."

That's a surreal thought, crashing for that long with someone I'm attracted to. But Derek doesn't seem perturbed by it. Once our sandwiches are made, the three of us flop onto Derek's sectional to eat. Travis and Derek are watching a TV show I haven't seen before, a crime thriller that they half-explain to me while chewing loudly. I pull out my phone, scrolling through real estate listings that haven't become any more auspicious since I looked at them earlier today. I switch to Twitter, where the main topic of discussion seems to be one of those advice posts asking if the person who wrote it is an asshole. One that makes me imagine my current situation.

Dear Internet, I hooked up with a hot colleague in order to get over my ex. A few months later, I got transferred to the same office as my hookup. Now I'm living with him while I search for an apartment in a saturated real estate market. Also, he's still blisteringly hot. Am I the asshole for taking a free room from a guy I hooked up with then left?

The answer is almost certainly yes. So when Travis and Derek are done eating, I offer to take their plates back to the kitchen.

A favor that doesn't make me feel much better about taking a room.

I return to the living room, but don't bother to sit again. Instead, I do an exaggerated yawn, then I make my excuses to go to bed. "Long day. See you tomorrow," I say.

Travis nods a friendly goodnight. "Catch you in the morning, Chason." A *ch* like church. I don't bother to correct him.

Derek cuts in. "It's Chason," Derek says, pronouncing my name correctly. I expect an eye roll from Travis, to be called *Chason* like *Chasing* just to be an asshole, the way some guys in the minors used to. Because ballplayers pick at each other, constantly, sometimes for funny stuff, sometimes for stuff that isn't as funny. I've learned to smile and say it doesn't bother me, even when it does, because sometimes that escalates. *Nice* doesn't pick fights in the clubhouse, even when guys deserve it. Besides, I'm not the only one with a name people can't seem to wrap their mouths around. Just ask Eugenio Morales on the Gothams. The broadcasters botch it more than they get it right. You learn to just deal with it.

"Like *Hazin'*, but the *H* is in your throat," Derek adds, maybe for my personal benefit.

Travis startles, clearly surprised at the correction. "My bad, Chason," he says to me. He can't quite manage the *ch*, a noise that proves tricky for ballplayers despite us all being experts in spitting. But it's not nothing, especially when Derek gives him an approving nod.

I murmur a *thanks*, not looking at Derek. Because his explanation makes something tighten in my chest. I like it—probably too much.

All the more reason I need my own apartment right away. If I throw my name around, I could get one fast. *Tomorrow*, I promise myself. *I'll start looking tomorrow.*

7

Derek

My first thought when big-mouthed Travis offered my spare room to the new guy was *Are you fucking kidding me?*

My second thought was about what Adam looks like rolling out of bed first thing in the morning.

I'm about to find that out.

I hope I don't regret it. I bought this place for its view—of the city skyline. And now of Adam, sitting at my kitchen island.

I'm not all the way awake yet. My "good morning" comes out hoarse.

For some reason, his cheeks go slightly red.

I wonder how far down that flush goes. Followed almost immediately by *Don't screw this up.*

Even if Adam probably blushes like he does most things—spectacularly. Which is endearing, and a little entertaining. His shy side makes me want to wind him up. And undo him in bed.

Not exactly a clubhouse leader thought. I definitely shouldn't be lusting after the guy living with me temporarily and working with me...for the foreseeable future.

But lusting after coffee?

Totally acceptable.

A cardboard carrying case holding two coffees sits next to him, along with various packets of sugar and cream.

He nods to the coffee. "Didn't know how you took it."

I suppress the urge to say, *Usually pretty enthusiastically.* Even without the retort, Adam turns a color Crayola would probably call *Mortification Red*.

Guessing he realized how he sounded. A little dirty. I don't entirely object.

"Sugar's good." I grab two packets, shake them, and dump them into my coffee. We're not going to make it through the week if we don't dial down the innuendo. Which I'll do.

Right now. Once I have caffeine. And breakfast. Maybe a workout. Possibly take a shower.

It's not entirely on me. Because are we ever going to acknowledge that he flirts his ass off with me—*but* also ran out of my house in Arizona? I'm not avoiding the riddle of my new roomie. I just don't know how to solve it. So I'm waiting for a more opportune time.

If there ever is one. "Thanks for the coffee," I eke out. *Kinda sucked when you pulled your pants on and left last time*, I don't say. Even if it was just a hookup. At least he was honest about it. I have no reason to feel this way, other than that I do. It'd be easier if he was an asshole. But Adam is actually this *nice*.

"No problem." Adam takes another sip of coffee, then clears his throat. "I was thinking about looking at some apartments later."

Oh. I hide my surprise with another drink. I wasn't expecting him to take off so soon. But that's his style. Too bad, since I want him gone for my sanity, I also kind of don't. This place is empty without someone else, ever since my last roommate, who was one of our relief pitchers, got traded in the Pilots' endless revolving door of players. Hearing Adam rustling around last night was nice. There's something oddly comforting about the low sound of the TV from another room, especially when that sound doesn't escalate.

"Where are you looking? Need any tips?" I ask. At least I can be helpful. He doesn't need to know I like the quiet company, especially since he's already got one foot out the door.

"Here." Adam thrusts his phone at me, as if to prove he's looking at listings. On it, a Zillow page. "What do you think?"

I take his phone, reading through the description of an apartment within an easy drive to the ballpark. Two bedrooms. A doorman. A state-of-the-art gym with an Olympic-sized pool. "Looks perfect." My lack of enthusiasm must show because he raises his very nice eyebrows in question. How are his eyebrows that attractive? Truly, I must be under-caffeinated.

"I was going to check it out tomorrow," he says. "If you wanted to come, that'd be cool." A small smile with that, one that I find more persuasive than I should. *He's your teammate. He left the night you sucked him off. And he might be taking your roster spot.* My muscles tighten. There—that's the resentment I should be feeling.

"Tomorrow sounds great," I manage.

Because the sooner he's out of here the sooner I can get back to normal. Nights alone. No one to bug me. Or lie to me about what he's up to. Perfectly alone. Which is definitely what I want.

We navigate the rest of the morning with limited contact. Adam goes to his room and I retreat to mine. He leaves the door open, even during a phone conversation: a call to his parents from the sound of it. They're talking about the trade, and he classifies me as *a buddy from the team who let me stay with him.*

I can't imagine calling my parents or stepparents. Certainly not having a long conversation with them. The last time I spoke with them was...Christmas, maybe. Shit, that was six months ago. I should probably set a reminder to check in every few months to make sure everyone's still all right. Or as all right as they get.

At least this year no one from the team bugged me about whether my dad would be coming on the annual "dads" trip for Father's Day, where all the dads, uncles, and grandpas travel with the team. If I get traded somewhere else, I'll have to go through telling the front office all over again. Yay.

Adam steps out of his room just as I'm

getting ready to head to the ballpark. "I was talking to my parents," he says. "They wanted to know when they can come see me play."

I know that's a thing parents do, but it always comes with a certain level of surprise. "Do they come to your games a lot?" I ask as I gather my wallet and phone from the living room.

He shrugs, but smiles. "As much as they can."

And he likes it. "Bet they cheer the loudest. Wave signs and all that."

He scratches his jaw, a little embarrassed. "Yes. That obvious?"

I hold up a thumb and forefinger. "Just a little. That's nice though. At least, it sounds like it is."

"I don't mind it," he says. The spark in his brown eyes says he not only doesn't mind it. He likes it.

I nod to the door, so we can take off. "So you really are Mister Wholesome?" Maybe teasing him will take my mind off my resentment.

He narrows his eyes. "I'm trying to be."

"You sure about that?" I prod.

His smile falters. He locks eyes with me, chin up. "Positive."

I swallow. I should stop. Truly, I should. There are a million reasons why messing around with Adam is a bad idea.

Starting with reason number one. *We play the same fucking position.* Doesn't take a genius to know what's coming next.

* * *

Once I reach the ballpark, our manager, Becker, calls me into his office.

"What's up, Skip?" I ask when I step inside.

"So, Miller, here's the thing," Becker begins, in his grizzled voice, looking like he's about to deliver the anvil drop I've been waiting for since Adam's trade was announced, trying to formulate whatever words will soften the blow.

My gut twists. I wish this weren't coming, but I pride myself on being a realist. I know the game too well to miss the signs—namely, how Adam's playing well. And how I've been playing well enough. I decide to make it easy on Becker. "Let me guess—you're moving me." I try to keep how I'm feeling out of my tone, though some must leak through.

"Second base," he confirms. "It could be

temporary." Though he says it in a way that means it probably isn't.

Great. Fucking fantastic. Turns out losing your spot sucks even when you see it coming. "Understood," I say, trying to take the news like a champ.

"You've played second before," Becker points out like that softens the blow. Which I have, though not since the minors. "We figured it'd give you some time to focus on your offense." A reminder that I'm having a down year, even if my "down" is better than a good chunk of the league.

"Yep," I say tightly, "got it." I grit my teeth, but try to shake off the annoyance as I trot out to the field. Maybe the sunlight will burn off some of my irritation. When I reach the diamond, Adam's taking ground ball practice.

That's annoying too.

If he looked good sitting in my kitchen earlier, he looks even better now, throwing while wearing a pair of baseball pants and a team T-shirt that shows off his toned body. When Adam spots me, he flashes me a grin, then scoops up the ball the coach sends to him like it's no harder than breathing. "Hey, Miller," he calls, "get out here."

I do, jogging out with a glove. The team's been patchwork about who's been playing second this year, so at least I'm not taking anyone's permanent spot.

"You up for practicing double plays?" he asks, as if he can tell I'm irritated about getting moved.

He doesn't press me when I just nod. I'm grateful for that.

Grateful too that he doesn't make a *thing* of it. He just wants to play ball. I know that feeling well. Baseball—it's reliable when nothing else is.

It does the trick today, loosening up the tension running up my back. I hope it works on some of the tension between us. I'll get over this. I always do. Doesn't hurt that Adam's too damn nice to be mad at. Too bad I like that about him.

Our first base coach hits balls to Adam, who turns, tossing them to me, and I throw on to Travis, who's set up at first. Hit-toss-catch-throw, hit-toss-catch-throw. Easy, the way the rest of the day hasn't been. Easier when Adam yells, "Good hands," after a particularly nice turn.

As I scoop the ball, and toss it his way, I serve the compliment back to him. "Same to you, Chason," I say.

And he gets a flush to his cheeks that has nothing to do with the grim Seattle weather.

Another reminder of that night.

He fights off a smile, but I can tell where his mind went.

I told myself I wouldn't linger on one quick hookup, but the way he acts around me—curious, flirty, and, let's be honest, really fucking interested makes me wonder if I was wrong about why he left.

Maybe he wasn't racing away from me.

Maybe he was running from whatever was happening in his life.

I might be reading something into nothing, but my instincts tell me Adam Chason thinks more about the night of the fundraiser than he ever expected.

And my instincts are rarely wrong.

But that doesn't mean I should act on them. I definitely shouldn't.

When we wrap up, Adam collects some of the balls littering the infield; I stay, gathering them up too. We're the only ones in earshot, the rest of the team having gone in to change for batting practice.

"Derek," he says, after a minute, softly, personally, getting my attention, "I didn't mean to displace you at short."

Something he doesn't have to say, but that deflates what remains of my previous temper. "It wasn't your decision."

"That's gotta be shitty, right? Guy comes in and takes your spot," Adam says. I can tell he legit feels bad.

"That's baseball. It's how it works," I say, trying to let him off the hook. "You wanna make it up to me?" I don't mean it sexually, but once the words make landfall, it's hard to hear them any other way.

Adam turns the same red he did this morning. A color I want to replicate, not on a baseball diamond, even if he's currently kneeling in the dirt. He looks my way, holding my gaze. His eyes glimmer with heat, the way they did that night. His desire flashes like a scoreboard in them. This is not the time and place. Yet, I can't resist teasing him. "If you really want to, that is," I add, and I don't bother to conceal the innuendo this time.

He breathes out hard. "I guess I owe you one."

Maybe he also regrets running off that night.

He bites the corner of his lips, and I stifle a groan. That look. That mouth. Everything about the last twenty-four hours makes me want to see if he looks just as good kneeling on my hard condo flooring. To do a lot more than that, none of which I should be thinking about in the middle infield.

"Maybe more than one," I say.

And I could be imagining his smirk as I jog off the field—but pretty sure I'm not.

8

Adam

Things I should do over the next few days—look for apartments.

Things I don't do—look for apartments.

In my defense, Derek's extra bed is really comfortable. I sleep better than I have in ages. Also, the coffee from the place around the corner is excellent.

I bang out a few emails to realtors, so points to me for trying.

Derek and I fall into a routine for the rest of our homestand. I get him coffee, we go to the park, we play ball.

And at night, Travis shows up, parking himself between us on the couch. Maybe his cockblocking ways are for the best. I don't trust myself to sit too close to Derek. But I truly don't have time to look for a place, because we take off for our series in Oakland against the Elephants. As I board the team jet, Audrey, one of the realtors I've messaged, pings me back. *I'd love to help you find a place. Thanks for sending over your must-haves. I'm assembling a list of available properties.*

She sends me times for an appointment. The first time that aligns is a day after our away series.

Which gives me a few more nights at Derek's condo.

Which I am enjoying far too much. Especially the shower. It's far enough away from him that when I blast some music, and take a long, hot shower, he can't hear me saying his name as I come.

* * *

We finish the series against the Oakland Elephants on Wednesday night, a game chilly enough I spend my time in the dugout warming my hands over a space heater. Alex Angelides, our catcher, is standing at the railing; he gives a slightly derisive snort as I rub my palms.

"How are you not freezing?" I ask.

"It's in the high fifties. Practically bathing suit weather." Because he's from New England—built broad and square, if a head shorter than most other guys in the dugout—he has opinions about the rest of us enduring the cold. Namely, that West Coast weather is warm and we're all wimps.

Who cares though, because Derek and I turn double plays like we've been doing it for years. One off a line drive I field from my knees, into the waiting cup of his glove. Another where he makes a diving grab, then flips it to me in a no-look throw at second before I send it on to first. I offer a hand up, a congratulatory whack of my glove against his ass as we walk off the field.

"Maybe *you* should be playing at short," I say then instantly regret it. Derek's been cool about this whole thing—cooler than I would have been if someone tried to take my spot in St. Louis—but I shouldn't make light of it either.

"Nah," he says breezily, "it's all yours."

No wonder he's a clubhouse leader. He called me *nice* but he's the one who has such a knack for what others need—a helpful word, a pat on the back, a smile, a joke, a serious piece of advice. I'm not sure who does that for him. Maybe no one. *Note to self: Move up that appointment with Audrey or you'll be sending heart emojis to your roomie.* Maybe I already am.

"I might want some reps at second," I say. My contract is up at the end of the year. Going into free agency with slightly more defensive versatility wouldn't be bad. If it means us working together, well...I don't hate that either.

He smiles. "You looking to switch it up?" Asked with an undercurrent I shouldn't be thinking about when I should be focused on my next at-bat. Or, really, thinking about during the game at all. "Definitely," I answer. I'm not talking about baseball positions though.

"Positional flexibility is really important," he says, solemnly, like ice wouldn't melt in his mouth. Except for his faint smirk. So he's not talking about baseball either.

We descend the dugout steps. I'm grateful for the chatty press of our teammates. I can't risk looking at him. Not when what I'm thinking is as obvious as the logo on my hat. *I want you.* All the things I can't say. "Agreed," I say, belatedly.

He draws an audible breath. "Good to know, Chason."

"Yeah, I'd say so."

And we've negotiated one of the most awkward and essential convos two guys need to have. Even though we can't do a thing about it.

Still, the good mood lasts as we change for the flight, load the bus to the airport, then ourselves onto the team jet. I answer my agent's texts as we wait for take-off.

Maddox: Tell me things. Is Seattle treating you right? Your stats seem to say so.

Adam: Can't complain.

Maddox: You never do. But seriously? Everything okay? Need help with anything? How's the living situation?

I turn toward the window, angling the phone so no one can see. He's not just my agent. He's a friend, so I write back with a little...hint.

Adam: Better than I expected. *A lot.*

Maddox: There's a story there, Adam. You'll tell me when I take you out to dinner next time I'm in town.

Adam: Maybe I will.

Even though I can't. Not the whole story. Right now, this hazy, warm feeling lasts through the flight and for the drive home to Derek's place. The easy vibe carries us up the elevator as we chat about the next series, down the hall as we talk about favorite players from years ago, to his front door as he slides in the key.

We're barely in the front hallway when he says, "You hear that?"

A telltale noise. A drip-drip-drip. Water.

We check the place, starting with the bathroom, and find nothing: no overflowing faucet or a running toilet. No issues in Derek's bedroom. I haven't been in here much, but it's as neat as always, homey with a big bed and a soft gray comforter.

Which means the noise must be coming from—*fuck*. My room.

When I walk in, the room looks okay, except for the center of the bed, which is soaked. Water drips steadily from the light fixture above it, leaving a splotch on the bedspread.

Great. Just what I want to come home to. *Home*, a word I'm not unpacking right now. And I feel bad that it's my room causing problems. "Sorry."

"Not your fault," Derek says, lightly. "I'll hit the breaker."

He leaves. A second later, there's a flicker, then the lights in the bedroom and bathroom power off. He returns, holding a pile of towels.

The bed makes a vague squelching noise as we strip it down. "What do you think did it?" I ask as I peel back the sodden sheets and toss them in the laundry basket.

"You're obviously cursed," he teases.

"Shut up," I say, smiling.

"I mean, seriously, you didn't need to apologize for a leak," he says. "Unless you planned it."

"Yep, you caught me." This must have been going on for a while, because the room smells vaguely mildewed. "For real, what do you think caused it?"

He shrugs. "Leaky pipe. Maybe the lady upstairs took one of those self-care baths and left the faucet running."

"Self-care bath?" I ask, because I'm sure he doesn't mean what I'm thinking.

Maybe he does because he laughs. "You know, candles, glass of wine, that kind of thing. I'm more of a shower guy."

I'd like to see his self-care in the shower.

"Yeah, big fan of showers myself too," I deadpan. Because as ballplayers we take an almost excessive number per day.

"I meant long ones, Chason." He smirks. "There's a rainfall fixture in mine if you ever want to check it out."

Which sounds like...an invitation.

"Anyway," he says, "I'll call maintenance in the morning."

I press my palm against the bed. It squishes. Yuck. "Mattress looks pretty well done for."

Derek presses his hand down too and cringes as water wells up. "This is *not* self-care."

"Definitely not. Guess I'm sleeping on the couch," I say, gesturing toward the living room—and my temporary bed.

His couch is comfortable by couch standards. Not if I'm going to spend a few days there while the leak gets fixed before I can get a new mattress. "Maybe there's a hotel nearby."

He scoffs. "Chason."

"Miller," I fire back.

He gives me that *you can't be serious* look, and oh shit. I know where this is going. I go hot all over.

"You can sleep with me," Derek says. As I expected and it still sends a jolt down my spine. "I've shared with guys before. In the minors. When we were traveling or whatever."

I have too but Derek isn't a random player I roomed with. "You sure?" I ask because I don't trust myself not to make this weird. I'm not going to pounce on him unwanted—more like once we get in bed, I'll be an open book. I'm sure my cheeks will flush, or my breath will hitch.

Or, more likely, I'll pop instant wood. I imagine it, the two of us pressed together—or more likely spending the night trying to stay apart through an unspoken agreement. Because *that night in Arizona* is on the list of things we're not talking about, even if we've talked about everything else.

Derek shrugs then answers lightly with, "We can sleep." As if something other than sleep could be on the menu.

Maybe it's just me wanting more.

I swallow, throat dry, then nod. "Okay."

I'm feeling less and less certain—trying to remember why hooking up with a teammate is a bad idea. None of those reasons feels particularly substantial now. *It'd make things... complicated*, I remind myself, even if spending a night in his bed already feels pretty complicated.

We clean up for another few minutes—Derek transporting my sodden bedsheets and towels to the washer, then finding a bucket somewhere to put under the drip. From there, we spend a normal evening, the two of us parked on the couch, but with the knowledge that, in a little while, we're going to sleep in the same bed. We watch...something. I couldn't tell you what if you paid me. A show of some kind, though I'm sure my eyes are seeing images on the screen and hearing sounds from the speakers. We're not sitting that far apart. His knee is very close to mine. Different from sliding up next to a dugout railing to talk about the game. Different from sitting near each other on the team jet. I glance down at where our legs are almost—not quite—touching.

Until Derek nudges his thigh against mine, and I startle more than is warranted. "Are you watching this?" he asks.

I blink at the TV screen like I'm seeing it for the first time. "Not really."

"Me neither." With that, a long yawn, maybe from genuine tiredness, since we're all tired at this point in the season. Or maybe he's as keyed up as I am and trying to cover it up.

I retreat to my darkened bedroom to change, pulling on sweats and a T-shirt, even if I mostly just sleep in my boxers.

When I get into Derek's room, he's scrolling on his phone, and he clearly had the same thought I did because he is—disappointingly—also wearing a shirt.

"Are you tired?" I ask. A couple-y question, even among guys living together for just over a week.

A shrug, a lift of one shoulder, and he's on top of the comforter, but soon he'll be under it. *We'll* be under it. Closer than we've been in a while but not quite close enough. "I'm ready to crash," he says.

"Cool. Me too." My mouth is dry. I should have brought a bottle of water. Something other than my phone and its charger, myself in gray sweatpants that conceal...well, I should get under the covers. Sooner rather than later.

Derek flips up the bedding and slides in. I follow. The lights are still on. It's awkward. For a second, we lie there, both still, bodies six inches apart, closer than we need to be. I can feel the heat coming off him in waves. He shifts. Our hands brush. And it's nothing—no different than our fingers overlapping when he hands me something in the kitchen or when we're doing defensive work out on the field. Nothing, except for how my breath can't seem to settle. How my mind supplies thoughts—specifically, of Derek on his knees smiling up at me challengingly—in a pulse like the persistent drip of water.

"Let me get the lamp." He clicks it off. The only light comes in through the uncovered window, the distant glitter of the city. We lie for a minute, breathing in the dark.

"It's been a while since I slept with someone," I say, then want to kick myself. Because what he doesn't need is a reminder of how I got up and left. "I mean…"

He laughs, slightly, a small ripple in the bedding. His sheets smell like him, like soap and the faint scent of rainwater cologne. "It's been a while for me too."

"Sorry," I say, a little anemically. "For leaving that night." The night we're not supposed to talk about, even if everything comes easier, here in the dark, with his thigh close to mine.

Like this confession. It's such a relief. I've wanted to say that for so long.

"It's all good," he says. "Though I was kind of surprised—you don't seem like the love 'em and leave 'em type."

He's so chill about it. But I sense his lightness is an olive branch—that he's giving me a pass on how I took off. I half wish the guy didn't make it so easy to like him.

But he is, so I turn toward him. "I'm not. My ex and I broke up right before spring training."

"You mentioned that. What happened?" he asks.

I laugh a little. "What didn't? Well, I got hit with the 'not sure how you're gonna marry me when you're in a committed relationship with baseball.' But it wasn't just that, you know?"

"Was she..." Derek trails off. A faint line develops between his eyebrows like he's thinking. "Is your ex also Jewish?"

A question that feels slightly adjacent to the one he actually wants to ask, the way he asked if any of my exes were men. "Talia? Yeah, she is."

"Is that important to you—that whoever

you date is Jewish?" Derek asks, a little thickly.

I smile. "It's not a requirement, no."

"Oh," Derek says. "Uh, good." Like he was asking hypothetically, even if my heart accelerates its beat against my ribs.

"How about you?" I ask. "What are you looking for?"

Derek's focusing on the ceiling, pensive. If he was handsome wearing a suit for casino night, and handsome on the ballfield, it's no match for how he looks here, in sweats, lit only by city lights.

"My last few relationships haven't exactly ended well," he says. "People told them I was gonna screw around on them. But it was kind of the opposite. Guess I really know how to pick 'em."

"That sucks."

He huffs a humorless laugh. "Don't I know it." Like it's no big thing.

Something that doesn't sit easily with me. "Whoever they are, they didn't deserve you." Then, with some consideration, I say, "I'm really sorry I left like that."

A brush of his shoulder against mine. "Well, you're here now."

"I am."

I want to reach across the covers, to pull

him close to me. To feel his weight on my chest, to let him kiss me into the mattress.

We stay where we are.

"You weren't how I thought you'd be," he says finally.

"You thought I'd be an asshole?"

"No. More, like you'd be fake. Like, no one could just be that *nice*, you know."

I want to nudge him but I'm not close enough to reach. "Says the guy who's letting me stay here rent-free and who gets the bread I like at the store."

Derek laughs. "Turns out I've been eating pastrami wrong for a while."

"White bread and mayo—who taught you to make it like that?"

"No one. I guess I taught myself growing up," he says with the slightly pinched expression he gets whenever the conversation drifts toward his home life, the details of which he seems reluctant to volunteer.

"You don't have to tell me…" I begin, but stop when he shakes his head.

"It's fine." Said in a way like it's not—not about me asking, but about the subject entirely. "My family wasn't exactly great growing up. I had to figure out a lot of stuff on my own. Mostly, I'm over it, but sometimes the smaller stuff gets to me."

"Like pastrami sandwiches?"

"Yeah, like that." Derek thinks for a minute. "Or like that I don't have to put up with someone if they cheat on me."

"The way your exes did?"

"Like that too. Like my parents did with each other. They're not together," he adds, then quickly shifts gears. "Anyway. It's no big deal you took off. Don't think twice about it."

But he's excusing me, and I don't want *that*. I want to own what I did. Be the guy I consider myself to be and make up for it.

"I do think about it," I say impulsively before I dwell on why this conversation is a risk. "A lot."

He swallows, his Adam's apple bobbing. He exhales slowly, maybe unsure if he should talk. Then he does, voice rough and hungry. "What do you think about that night?"

I already tapped the door open, I might as well kick it all the way.

I push up on an elbow. "How much I want another," I say, and the admission both frees me and turns me on.

Derek parks his hands behind his head, lets a slow smile take shape, then murmurs, "How much, Chason?"

And I hear my last name all the time—hollered on the field and across the clubhouse—but usually without such...care. A rumble, like he practiced it. I want to hear him say it with his hands threaded through my hair. "Want me to show you?"

Derek turns to me, his smile wicked. "Yeah. I do. So show me. Show me now."

The tension of what we're not talking about vanishes, replaced by a greater one: pure lust and risk...but one I want to take as I reach for his face, then erase the distance between us.

Before, in Arizona, I felt like my clothes would burn off into the cooling desert night. Now, a different kind of urgency drives me as I run my knuckles over his stubbled jaw, a more intimate kind, as our bodies press together under the covers.

I'm a little impatient, and a lot eager, so I don't tease or toy. I take his mouth, kissing him deeply, insistently. His hands come up to my shoulders, and I heat up everywhere, not slowing down. Not when he gasps as I bite his lip. Not when I run a hand down his arm, to his side, around to his ass. Yanking him closer. We rub together, seeking friction through all these clothes. Too far away from each other.

All at once, I want everything.

Us naked, tangled together. Kissing and fucking and not stopping at all.

But I don't want to end this kiss. This deep, dizzying kiss. He kisses the way he plays baseball—with fierce determination. With intensity. With all his focus poured into me.

Then he slides a hand between our chests, presses hard on my pecs, pushes me off.

I blink. "Why did you stop?"

His knowing smile makes my cock even harder. "Tell me what you want."

What do I want? Isn't it obvious? I want to touch him. I don't want to stop touching him. But I flash back to the night he got on his knees for me.

Just wanted to hear you say suck me off.

Derek Miller is under my skin, and in my head, and he's unlocking me.

I'm the guy who walks into an event and hopes he doesn't have to say a word. In bed, Derek wants me to talk.

I let the full weight of the statement press into me, as I grab his shoulder, pull him on top of me. Then, I rope my hands in his hair, tug on the strands, dragging out a groan from him.

I've had a lot of time to think about what I

want. Months, really. Definitely since I moved in. And absolutely since I got into bed with him.

Now I just need to say it.

"I want to make it up to you."

His smile is warm, heated. "What's that?"

Feeling daring, I whisper, "Let me suck you." A nod, an urging of his hips. I tug at him to keep him close. "I wasn't done yet," I say. "I want you to fuck my throat. And maybe when you get all worked up, you can throw me on this mattress and fuck me."

The spark in his eyes is worth everything.

9

Derek

Yes, please.

And now.

Holy fuck. I didn't know I had a big thing for shy guys who are filthy talkers in bed till now.

But maybe I just have a big thing for my teammate.

And right now, one other thing is very big. Adam slides my sweats off my hips, then pauses, hand at the waistband of my boxer briefs. He swallows, then says, "I may have been overambitious."

I sit up, resting my weight on my elbows.

As turned on as I am, his hesitation makes me apprehensive.

Until he shrugs, then adds, "I don't mind a challenge."

I laugh. "Feels like there's a compliment in there."

He runs a hand over my cock, the scratch of cotton the only thing keeping me grounded. "There was," he confirms, as I sit up and rip off my shirt.

"Let me get these," he says, a shyness flashing on his features, till it disappears when he tugs off my briefs.

A long groan fills my room as he stares at me.

"Been thinking about this for a while," Adam whispers.

I lie back on the pillow, wrap a hand through his soft hair. "How long?"

"A few months and three nights, give or take," he says.

"Then get your mouth on me," I urge.

"Thought you wanted me to talk."

"Moaning is a form of talking." Now that we're here, naked, with him looking at me like that, I don't want to make promises I can't keep. Like I won't come down his throat. Or that we can do this again.

He slides down between my legs, gives my

dick a few pumps, then takes me into his mouth, tongue playing with the foreskin. "Fuck yes," I mutter, and once I say that, he's sucking hard.

I'm learning all sorts of things about Adam tonight. He likes to talk in bed, and he likes to listen. Since his mouth is occupied, I'll handle the chit-chat. "Take me deeper," I murmur, gripping his head tighter with one hand.

He obeys, sucking my cock with a concentrated fervor, quickly finding a rhythm that sends tingles down my legs.

"Harder," I encourage, pushing my hand on his shoulder, helping him along.

Adam moans around my dick, and that's the hottest thing ever. His sounds. Except, wait. I'm wrong. He's humping the bed as he sucks me off. *That* is scorching.

So sexy in fact, I'm worried this will be over too soon. I indulge in a few more of his deep, purposeful sucks. But the second my balls tighten, I pull him off.

"Get your clothes off now," I say.

He hops off the bed, and sheds his pants, shirt, and boxers in seconds flat. "Will that do?" he teases.

"Mmm. That'll do just fine," I say as I stare at his body, long enough that he flushes down his chest. *Knew it.* "Get up here."

He climbs on me, straddling me, as responsive to commands as he is to being touched.

I drag my hands down his chest, through the smattering of hair. "Is this when I throw you on the mattress?"

The shudder that runs through him is ridiculously sexy.

I grab his hips, make him grind against me, his hard cock thumping against mine.

"Or maybe . . ." Adam says, then trails off. He's so turned on he can't speak. That won't do.

I sit up higher. Brush my lips to his. Taunt him with a tease of a kiss, with my fingers wrapping briefly, unsatisfyingly, around his cock "You want me inside you?"

He nods, apparently wordless. That won't work.

"You can have my cock"—I stroke him again—"when you tell me *exactly what you want*."

His eyes flutter open. They glimmer with heat. "I want to ride you."

I laugh. I can't help it. He's so surprising in bed, and I fucking love it. "Good."

But first, I move him off me, and grab

supplies from the nightstand drawer. I take my turn between his legs, playing with his cock, as I lube up my fingers. But I stop before I go any farther. "Tell me."

"Open me up." He takes in a ragged breath. "So you can fuck me."

A tone like the press of his heels into the mattress, like the subtle shake in his arms. Like he's desperate for it. I don't make him wait any longer. When I've got him panting and moaning, I drop my face to his dick, suck on the leaking head, then sit up.

"Fuck, Derek. I'm so turned on," he says, sounding lost in a haze.

"Good." I kiss him, hard, then flop to my back, roll on a condom, and coat it once more with lube. "Now get on me."

Adam complies, straddling me, his strong body rising over me, and holy hell, what a view.

He reaches for my covered cock and guides me in. Slowly, taking his time. A wince, then a blissed-out smile.

I blow out a measured breath as his heat squeezes my dick. Nice and tight. Pleasure rushes up and down my body. Everywhere.

Adam closes his eyes. He's smiling as he rocks on me, like he wants to figure me out. It's been a long time since someone cared enough to do that, to treat me like some kind of brand-new discovery. He swivels his hips just so, then opens his eyes.

"That feel good?" I ask.

A frantic nod. He exhales long and deep, then presses his hands against my chest. "Gonna fuck your cock," he whispers.

I am electrified. This man is shocking me in the best of ways. I curl my hands around his hips, guiding him along. "Ride me hard," I command.

So, he does. Fucking, and rocking, and bouncing.

Our words fade away, replaced by grunts and groans. By sweat and heat. By this unexpected connection between him and me as he finds me in the dark.

I'm on edge the whole time, muscles tight, skin sizzling. I hold on, watching his every move, wanting to make it so good for him. When he reaches for his cock, gripping it tight, the pleasure in me threatens to tip over.

"Gonna come all over you," he says, and I can hear the thrill in his voice. Not just from the orgasm, but from *the announcement*.

"Make a mess of me," I encourage, staring at his face twisting in pleasure, the drop of sweat sliding down his chest, and his hand, flying on his cock, till he grunts, and spills all over me.

I'm seconds behind him, the night spinning away as I follow him, coming hard. And then feeling something new as he leans down, brushes a soft kiss to my lips.

I kiss him back the same way. Tender and close.

* * *

A little later, after we clean up, I'm sure there are words we should say. Like *We can't do this again* or *That was a one-time thing* or *What happens tomorrow?*

But after the flight, after the water leak and the way we fucked, I don't want to think about tomorrow.

I want to *enjoy* this night.

He looks slightly unsure when he returns from the bathroom, like he doesn't know if he'll be invited back to bed. Like I'm going to send him to the couch or a nearby hotel as repayment for how he ran out during spring training. A wariness I understand even if it's not warranted.

I pat the bed. "Don't put your clothes back on," I say.

Adam gets back under the covers, a few inches apart, closer than the first time.

He yawns, sounding content, and I love the sound. Then he lifts his hand, slides it down the ink on my chest, tracing the sunburst then the stars. "What are these for? I wanted to ask the first night."

A personal question. One I've answered reluctantly for others. One that maybe reveals too much about me. But I think, and I hope, Adam will understand in a way others probably haven't. "Baseball," I say.

He frowns, confused. "How?"

"It centered me. It felt like the sun," I say, admitting a scary truth of my soul. I love the game. "It's my constant. Like the sun and the stars."

He's quiet for a second, then he moves over me, kisses the sun, then the stars, then settles next to me. I have no idea where we're going tomorrow, but for tonight, I'll take everything he's offering.

Especially when he says, "I get it."

That's the best part of this thing with him. But that's the problem too.

10

Derek

When I wake up the next morning, the sheets beside me are cold. *Again?* My guard is up as I leave my bedroom, expecting to find Adam just gone. Old habits. Protective habits. People leave. They just do.

Instead, he's seated at the kitchen island, dressed, with coffees in a cardboard holder next to him. His face is apprehensively scrunched as he reads his phone. Not a great morning-after look, even if I feel the same way.

Unsure what happens next. Or what *should* happen next.

"Good morning," I say.

"Same to you," he says.

He doesn't move to kiss me. Shame. "We should probably talk," he says instead.

We should. I know we should. It'll just suck. "Yeah," I say, bracing myself for bad news. How the fuck have I gotten to this point with him in such a short time? I should just shrug him off. But I can't seem to, and that's irritating. I wish he weren't under my skin.

"Last time, we weren't that clear with each other," he says.

"We weren't," I say, letting him take the lead.

"I really like you," Adam begins, and I look away so he doesn't see the stupidly big grin coming from his admission. But I can also sense a *but* coming on the horizon. "But I probably shouldn't live here," he adds.

Ohhhh.

That's not the *but* I expected. Maybe he was fooling me twice and running out the door again. But I get where he's coming from though. We probably don't need to go from zero to sixty overnight. I turn back to him. "Yeah," I say, a little defeated.

"It makes things complicated," he says.

"It does, and they're already complicated," I add, then I swallow some too-hot coffee. Because where he lives is fixable.

Where he works got a little more permanent when he joined the Pilots. "Same team and all."

Adam nods. "That would seem to be the problem."

"It does."

"If things were different..."

It's my turn to laugh at the irony of our situation. "You mean, if we weren't on the same team."

Adam's eyes soften, and fuck, this would be so much easier if he wasn't *nice* and mature. And also *correct* that we can't just slide into a relationship. Even if we both want to.

"Audrey—my realtor—sent me a list of places," he says. "One's available today if you want to come see it with me." A couple-y errand I don't want to decline, even if we're not going down that road.

"Sure. Let me call maintenance first," I say, "then we'll take off."

Adam smirks.

I tilt my head.

His eyes travel up and down my frame. I'm only in boxer briefs. I smile at the same time he does.

"Maybe get dressed too," he says drily.

"This is what I usually wear when I look

for apartments. It doesn't work for you?" I tease.

His smile turns big. Then he rises, cups my chin. "Totally works for me," he whispers hotly against my mouth. Then he dusts his lips across mine. Mmm. A shiver runs down my spine. The taste of coffee mixed with Adam first thing in the morning is too damn tempting.

When he breaks the kiss, he looks a little dizzy.

Damn, he's making this whole find-separate-places-thing hard. But the living arrangement issue is the smaller issue.

I need to remember the bigger one.

* * *

Later that morning, we drive a mile away to a gleaming apartment building that reflects the clear summer sky. After we park, Audrey meets us in the lobby, holding a leather portfolio and sporting an *I'm ready to do business* grin.

She strides up to Adam first. "Great to meet you. Glad we could find a time," she says, then hands him a printout. After a second, she hands me one as well.

"All the details about the apartment specs," she says.

I take it, because it's not my job to say *I'm not the buyer*. But I find it amusing. And I kinda want to see what Adam will say.

I'm not sure what Adam told her about himself—that he's a ballplayer looking for his own place? Or who she assumes I am—a friend, probably. A boyfriend, possibly.

But Adam's not quiet for long. He squares his shoulder. "This is..." In slow motion he turns to me, his cheeks splashed with heat. In a heartbeat, I know he's thinking of last night. Trying to find a definition for what we were, what we are.

It's borderline entertaining. I *could* put him out of his misery, but it's a little too fun.

"I'm his current landlord," I say innocently.

He snorts, shaking his head in amusement. "And driver," he adds.

A crease forms in Audrey's brow, then smooths. "You're Derek Miller."

"Nice to meet you." I offer my hand.

Audrey shakes it. "Okay, let me show you upstairs."

As she heads across the lobby, I hang back. "You could have told her I'm the guy who made you come hard last night," I whisper.

Adam rolls his eyes.

I shrug happily. "Can't argue with the truth."

He steals a glance at me as we reach the elevator. "True. You can't."

We follow Audrey up a long elevator ride to an apartment near the top floor. Once inside, she sweeps out an arm. "Why don't you both look around? I'll be here to answer any questions."

She hangs back as we explore.

The place is nice, though with little in the way of personality beyond the floor-to-ceiling windows in the living room that'll likely provide a good view of the rain for most of the year. We find ourselves staring out of them. Adam's hands are balled in his pockets the way he does when he's unsure.

The light mood of the lobby slips away.

The reality of his moving out hits me. That I've gotten used to him being around all the time and will be sad to see him gone. I peer at the open concept living room-slash-dining room. "This place might echo, given all the space."

Adam doesn't point out that my condo is laid out the same way. "I can get rugs."

I nod to the windows letting in a stream of mid-morning light. "Might get too bright in here."

His lips twitch. "In Seattle?"

"You never know. Let's check it out one more time?" I suggest.

We do another lap of the apartment. The more I look at this place, the more it won't suit a ballplayer. We need curtains to sleep late, thick walls to cover up parties. Some place like my condo. When we return to the living room I ask, "Do you think this would work for you?" I don't want to say *This place is all wrong for you. Unlike mine.* I'll sound like I'm trying to apartment-block him. A new form of cockblocking where you don't let your too sexy, too sweet, too thoughtful roomie move out even though you should.

Audrey coughs politely, reminding us she's there. "What do you think, Adam?"

"Not sure this one is right for me," Adam says.

I can't tell if that's because I said something or if he truly doesn't like it. Now I feel slightly guilty for bad-mouthing the place. Audrey gives him a professional smile. "I totally understand. We'll keep looking till you find the right one. Bear in mind the market's pretty aggressive right now."

"That's what I've heard." Adam looks around at the wood floors and high ceilings one more time. "It's just that generally I like to know a place a little better before I commit."

"There's a good chance it won't be available if you take your time. No pressure. But we do need to remember that," she says.

Adam frowns, like he's been called out by a teacher for wasting the class's time. "Would it be helpful if I gave you a clearer list of what I'm looking for?"

She nods, overeager. "A more detailed list would be very helpful." And he smiles at that, until she adds, "Perhaps one both of you contribute to."

I blink.

Adam flinches. But he glances at me for a hot second, looking equal parts amused and abashed. Then he turns back to her. "Of course. We can make a list," Adam assures her.

"If you're not ready to decide, I have another couple coming to see the place later who are in a hurry to buy," she says. *Another couple*. Neither of us corrects her.

I don't want to.

I hope that's his excuse too.

Audrey shows us two more places. Adam

finds something wrong with one of them. I find something wrong with the other one.

And we go to the ballpark for a game with no more prospects than we started with. But at least we win the game.

11

Adam

That night at Derek's condo, I deal with reality.

Three failed apartments today.

And it was my damn idea to look for one ASAP. I'm the one who said this morning *I need to move out*.

But what did I do? I stalled. I came up with reasons each place was wrong.

The pathetic truth? The thought of leaving Derek twists me up. Makes me feel empty. A ridiculous thought. I've only been here a short while. I shouldn't feel this way. I shouldn't miss him before I even leave.

But as I park myself at the barstool at the

kitchen island, with a notepad in front of me, my phone next to it, I face the reality of my feelings—I'll miss what we could have had.

I'm dawdling because once I leave, there are no more excuses. I want to date him. I want to go out to dinner with him. To play golf. To see a football game.

But I can't. So I force myself to deal with the list of my housing preferences. As he roots in the fridge, I tap my pen against the blank notepad.

"You wanna help me make a list?" I ask.

He glances at me from the fridge. "I'm surprised you don't have one already," he says.

"Do I seem like a list guy?"

Derek's blue eyes twinkle as he grabs a beer. "You sure do."

Like that, he busts me, and I like it. "Fine. I do—well, I did, but you brought up a few things that I wouldn't have thought of, so I thought I'd make another."

"How organized," he says, uncapping the darker brew he favors, then he grabs a lighter one for me.

"Fine. It's my second attempt," I admit, taking the bottle. "Thanks."

"Anytime," he says.

I wish.

That's the problem. I keep wanting more. I really need to get out of here. The longer I drag things out, the harder I'll fall for him. After I open my beer, he tips the neck of his bottle toward mine. "To being organized," he says, then eyes the conspicuously blank paper. "What are you looking for?"

I shift slightly on the stool. This feels personal. But I don't hate picking out a place with his input, partly because it's about planning for the future. It makes Derek seem more like a boyfriend than a teammate. "Couple bedrooms. Definitely a spare room in case my parents or sister decides to visit."

"So two or three bedrooms. For family," he says, lips twitching. He enjoys that I'm close with them. "Got it. What else?"

"You always talk about the lighting. I guess I never noticed that before," I say.

"Probably because St. Louis gets more than five sunny days a year."

"True. But I don't miss the sunny days," I say. Already I like Seattle better. For lots of reasons. Not just winning.

On the list I jot down *Moderate lighting.*

"There. We like lighting," I say, before I realize my faux pas. I said that like I'm picking out an apartment for both of us. "I mean, I do."

He smiles. "I do. We do. We can both like it...*Chason*," he says, then comes around the island and sits next to me. Closer than a friend would. It'd be nothing to reach over and kiss him, like he did with me this morning. To fold ourselves together.

But if I kiss him, I won't want to stop. Kissing won't make it easier to move out. Or be *just* teammates.

I force my focus back to the list, my grip tightening around the pen. "What else do I want?" I ask. My voice sounds hoarse to my own ears. I grab my bottle, take a drink. But my throat still feels dry.

Derek lifts a brow. "I don't know, Adam. What else do you want?"

You.

"What should I be looking for in an *apartment*?" I clarify.

"You like a big kitchen."

I tap my pen top. "Sure."

"Since you have a lot of opinions about food."

I laugh. "Yeah, I've heard that."

"You like to take long showers," he adds, a little playful, then takes a drink of his beer. "So good water pressure."

But I stop at the word *long*. "You noticed I

take long showers?" His eyes darken as he sets down the bottle. "I did."

Heat slides down my chest. "Why did you notice?"

He reaches across the island. Takes my pen. Sets it down. Licks the corner of his lips. "Because I had to fight to not go in there with you."

I burn up everywhere. I lean closer. "Don't fight it now."

* * *

The rainfall shower beats down on me. I'm alone, hair slicked, soaping up. Doesn't matter that I showered before we left the ballpark. Don't need this shower to get clean.

I tip my head back in the dim lighting of the big bathroom. When the door creaks open, a spark shoots down my legs. My cock hardens. The thought of Derek discovering me is a wicked thrill, even though we planned this moments ago.

I close my eyes. Loosely, I grip my cock, stroking it once under the water. Seconds later, the glass door to the shower opens.

Derek growls before he speaks. A low, dirty rumble as he joins me. He doesn't touch me and I don't open my eyes. I just slow down.

"Mmm, don't stop on my account," he says.

"I won't," I murmur, my fist sliding up my shaft, twisting at the head.

"Definitely wanted to walk in on this," he says.

"You should have," I whisper, fighting off the wish that he could do this tomorrow, the next day. I focus on the here and now. "What would you have done?"

He answers me without words, lips crashing down on mine. A hard, possessive kiss. Then he drags his hand between our stomachs, down to my cock.

"Enjoyed you," he answers, taking over, wrapping his fist around the base.

Those two words echo painfully. This man does *enjoy me*. He seems to savor every second touching me. His indulgence is another thing I'll miss.

But I don't want to think about what I'll miss. I want to have him one more time.

I open my eyes, then reach for him, nudging him toward the wall.

"What do you want tonight?" Derek breathes.

"I want you," I say, loud, over the sound of

the water. In a way that doesn't come easily to me until it does. "Want to make us both feel so fucking good."

His smile erases. "Do it."

I reach for his thick cock, then stroke up. He shudders the second I touch him with my slicked-up hand. I tighten my fist, savoring his reaction. The flare in his nostrils. The harshness in his breath.

Then, as I go faster, the helplessness in his sounds. "Fuck, I'm not gonna last long," he mutters.

"Good," I say roughly, strangely surprised at the intensity of my voice.

Derek's eyes widen. "Finish us together."

I push closer, our chests touching, our cocks rubbing. His lips part, a tell-tale sign he's close.

And yes, I *want* to jerk us together, but this may be my last chance to taste him. My *only chance.*

I drop down to my knees. I don't owe him one, but maybe I owe myself this. A chance, however fleeting, to make it up to him. Instantly, he curls his hands around my hair.

"Oh fuck, yes," he says.

His excitement trips all my wires.

It makes me feel proud and aroused at the same time.

I wrap my hands around his ass, squeeze him, urging him into my mouth, to use me to get off.

"If you could talk I bet you'd say *fuck my face* right now," he says.

Holy fuck. I would. I shudder and nod my yes.

"Yeah, I knew you would," he says, then he delivers. Thrusting in a few quick pumps till he's coming down my throat.

Then while he's still moaning, still panting, he reaches for my hands, pulls me up, and guides me against the wall.

"Won't take long," I whisper, as he wraps a hand around my dick. In no time, I'm losing touch with reality, pleasure taking over, as I come hard in his hand, on his stomach.

And I love everything about this shower fantasy.

Far too much.

12

Adam

In the morning, my phone rings obnoxiously.

From the other side of the apartment.

Oh shit.

I bolt up, race out of Derek's bed—I seriously cannot stop sleeping with him—and skid into the kitchen, grabbing my phone from the counter. After we showered last night, I was in the kitchen sending my list to Audrey, then abandoned my phone when Derek was hungry. *For round two.*

Me bending him over his bed. We both enjoyed that as much, if not more, than the shower.

Another ring. I slide the call open fast.

"Hey, Audrey." I keep my voice low since I don't want to wake Derek.

"Hi, Adam. Good news," she chirps, as I pad to the living room, farther away from our —*Derek's*—bedroom. "I have a potential place for you."

Wait, what? "You do? Already?"

"Your list was helpful. Thanks for sending it last night. I really appreciate the details. And yes, I have a fantastic three-bedroom, with terrific lighting, a rainfall shower in the main bedroom, and a big kitchen. It's everything you want," she says, then rattles off the address.

It's...this building's twin. Literally. It's owned by the same company. It's two blocks away.

Holy shit.

As she talks, I pop in earbuds and look up the place on my phone. I open the listing and whistle quietly in appreciation. It's a great apartment.

"The windows are terrific—you'll have a great view of Lake Union," she says as I flick through the pictures.

The apartment is everything I want.

With one tiny exception. It's not *this* place. Where I am right now. Which is exactly why I have to take it. "How soon can I move in?" I ask even though the question rips at my chest.

"That's the best part. It's vacant. So, how's today?"

"Perfect," I choke out.

As she shares the details, the sound of footsteps on hardwood floors grows louder. I turn and my breath catches. Derek's yawning, scratching his hair and I want to freeze time. Sleepy sexy Derek is my new favorite look.

And this is the last morning I'll get to see it.

When Audrey finishes a minute later, I thank her, then hang up. I trudge into the kitchen to the end of the most unexpected and bittersweet romance in my life.

I shouldn't be so hung up on him.

We only spent over a week together. But I've never felt so understood. So wanted.

Yet, everything is happening too soon. The trade, these feelings, moving. *Everything*. What if I can't balance it?

It's not the first time I've tried to do too much. *Talia*. Derek and I will reach an inevitable end—and then I'll have to see him every single day at the ballpark.

"Derek," I say, his name scraping my throat.

The guy I like far too much cranes his

neck from the fridge. "She found you a place," he says evenly.

I blink. How the fuck did he do that? "Did you hear me on the phone?"

Shaking his head, he gives a sad smile. At least, I think it's sad. Maybe I just hope it is. "I kind of figured it out from the look on your face," he says, waving at me.

It hurts breaking things off with someone I feel like I've known for longer than the time we've had together.

"I can move in when I want. It's two blocks away. And this is wild—it's basically the same layout. The same place. A sister building," I say. All the words topple from my mouth at once, and crash land in a mess so I don't say something I'll regret. Like *I don't want to leave because I'm falling for you. Or I have to go since I don't want to get too caught up in you. But you get it, right? Your tattoos say you do. Baseball is your constant. Well, it's mine too.*

Maybe I don't have to say anything because he closes the distance, cups my chin and says, "We always knew this was temporary. But it was good while it lasted, *Chason*."

It was great.

He'd called me Adam last night. I'm back to my last name. To being a teammate, a friend. "Yeah, it was," I say, trying to play it nonchalant too. "I had fun."

"Me too," he says. His tone is light, though that might just be for my benefit. "And now we'll get back to work."

He lets go of my face, returns to the fridge and grabs the carton of eggs, then sets to work making his breakfast. Saying nothing.

"Do you want me to get coffee?" I ask awkwardly.

With his back to me, he shakes his head. "I'm all good."

Maybe he's good. But I'm not. And that —*him* saying he's chill, me being a wreck inside—is why I turn around and pack my bags so damn fast.

13

Derek

A week or so later, I open the door to my condo after a game.

I brace myself.

Every time I've walked in here since he left, I've been clobbered by a wave of feelings. *Missing.*

At least it doesn't smell like a cabin anymore. Maintenance fixed the leak and hauled away the sodden mattress too.

So I've got my spare bedroom back, complete with an empty bed frame to match the hollowness in my chest.

Good times.

I shut the door, flop down on my couch,

and grab the remote. I'm not in the mood to watch anything, so I pick up my phone and open my e-reader. I click on a thriller I downloaded the other week. Maybe Axel Huxley's international tales of intrigue will take my mind off this annoying ache in my heart. His latest book does the trick for a few chapters, the story helping me escape these feelings that aren't going anywhere.

Until the moment's broken by a loud, presumptive knock at my front door. *Travis*.

I flash back to the last time he popped by, when Adam was still living—staying—here. *Not helpful*.

I shove the memory away as I head to the door, answer it and let Travis in, even though I saw him an hour ago. "Aww, you miss me," I tease, trying desperately to keep my mood light.

Since it's easier than admitting the truth. I needed company tonight. Badly.

Sure, sometimes it's annoying how Travis invites himself over and eats his way through my fridge. But he's a good guy, a solid ballplayer, and I'm grateful that he's here. I pull out food from the fridge. Rye bread, mustard, pastrami. Adam's right—the sandwich is better this way.

My heart twinges once more, and again

that's not helpful—all these reminders of him.

I force myself to focus on sports. "That was a helluva game tonight," I say as I toast the bread.

"Sure was. You're doing well at second. Man, I can't imagine having to switch like that."

"Because you play first," I say drily.

"I believe my bat reflects that, thank you very much." He puffs out his chest.

He's not wrong. He anchors the lineup for a reason. "Yes, it does," I say, no teasing this time. "And thanks for the compliment."

"You played second in the minors?"

"I did. I guess I didn't forget it all," I say as I spread mustard on the bread. Truthfully, switching to second is working partly because my best skill might be adaptability. Bumping back and forth between my parents' houses as a kid, spending some nights alone, hiding under the covers with the dog when the shouting got to be too much—I had to adapt.

Which is what I've had to do on the diamond. When I finish making the sandwich, I slide it in front of Travis. "One pastrami for you," I say.

He smiles, takes a bite, then swipes the

mustard off his mouth. "Dude. This is the Adam-style," he says.

And it's like a punch in the gut.

Like I don't have enough reminders of the guy at the park.

"Yes," I say tensely.

"Should we bring him one? At his new place? It's not far."

I do want to see his place. But I'm sure I'd like the lighting too much for my own good.

I make a show of yawning. "I'm gonna crash soon. But feel free," I say, then turn, so he can't see the longing on my face.

* * *

Days snap back to their pre-Adam rhythm over the next several weeks. I go to the ballpark. I play. We're playing good baseball, maybe better than we have in years. Adam's no different in the clubhouse—quiet, thoughtful—or on the field, where all his shyness seems to melt away.

Missing someone you see every day is great. *Said no one ever.*

What's actually great is that it's been several weeks since my last fielding error. In the seventh, Adam lobs a grounder to me and we turn a flawless double play. He flashes a smile. "Looking good," he says as we head off the field.

I smile too, wishing I felt it entirely.

But I *do* feel better when I reach the dugout and Becker claps me on the back. "You're taking to second like a natural, Miller," he says. From him, that's high praise.

"Thanks, Skip."

There's that, at least. My game has improved. I've handled this transition. I've adapted. I've needed to do it so I have. That's what I fucking do.

Maybe I needed to get Adam out of my home.

Maybe I need to keep focusing on the game—and not on the way I feel when I return to my condo and I'm alone again.

14

Adam

My new apartment is great. Plenty of light, but not so much glare it wakes me. Neighbors who don't seem concerned that I'm going to throw wild parties—but to be fair, I'm not. It also allows for dogs up to sixty pounds so I spend a lot of time looking at listings from a local shelter, even though having a dog and being on the road will be tough. But a man can dream.

And I do since this place is great. Really.

Except for the mattress I bought online, which is either too hard or too soft. Or maybe the problem with my bed is that it doesn't have Derek in it.

At least we're on the road half the time, the grind of the baseball season a welcome distraction from the conspicuous distance between Derek and me. Guys notice—Travis attempts something like a heart-to-heart on a flight to Houston that I manage to mostly avoid.

It's harder to avoid Angelides, our catcher, who approaches the empty seat next to mine on the plane ride back, giving me a grunted "Anyone sitting here?" and not waiting for an answer before dropping down.

We haven't interacted that much since the trade—he's usually got a cloud of anger around him that matches any slate-y Seattle day, though he's easy enough to work with on the field.

I wait for him to say what he wants—maybe to talk about fielding. Maybe his usual seat was just taken.

"You good?" he asks, eventually, a question that can encompass a lot.

"Do I seem not good?"

A shrug of one of his thick shoulders. Then a patient silence.

I study the airport tarmac out the window, shimmering with mid-summer heat.

Angelides doesn't say anything. The

silence is growing awkward, probably purposefully.

"I'll be fine," I say.

"If something's going on in the clubhouse or off the field"—Angelides makes a hand gesture that could encapsulate a lot of things—"better to deal with it directly than let it go."

Said like he knows that from experience.

"Stuff can get complicated," I say. There. Nice and vague.

"And sometimes guys pretend to be cool about stuff they're not actually cool with," Angelides counters.

Busted. But this isn't just my business to tell. And the stuff with Derek—I'll get over it.

"Thanks, man," I manage. "I'll give that some thought."

Angelides nods. For a second, I worry he's going to press the point. Instead he gets up, then claims an empty row nearby, leaning against the plane window. A brief expression passes over his face—eyes scrunched shut momentarily as if in regret—before he settles in to sleep.

I have the rest of the plane ride to think about the situation with Derek. I'm sure we'll return to being real friends, instead of two guys making small talk. For now everything between us feels too recent, too fresh.

Like when we land and go our separate ways at the airport. I wish I were hopping into his car to head to his place. Instead, I go to mine.

Eventually, once I have furniture and my apartment looks like a human being—or at least a ballplayer—lives in it, my parents demand a tour.

"So, let us see the place," my mother says, when I FaceTime them one morning in August.

I point my phone camera at the sparkling clean countertops in the kitchen. They're pristine because I've mostly been eating team-provided food and I haven't been making late-night sandwiches.

Then I show them the couch where I've been occupying the middle cushion because there's no one else to sit on it. The windows admitting the late morning Seattle light.

"It has a pretty good view," I say, and hold up the camera so they can see the city—or possibly just the glare off the windows. *Maybe Derek's looking at the same view.* Which is too melodramatic a thought for eleven in the morning, when we'll see each other in a few short hours.

"Not too much light?" my dad asks. Because they know I usually sleep until midmorning.

"No," I say, "the lighting's perfect." My throat goes faintly scratchy. I know why and there's nothing I can do about it.

"And you're liking Seattle?" my mom asks.

My throat goes even tighter. "Seattle's great. Really. Everything's going better than I expected."

When I put it that way, it doesn't even sound like a lie.

* * *

A few days later, my mattress situation shifts from an inconvenience to an actual problem when I wake up with a twinge in my back. The discomfort lasts through a shower, my drive to the ballpark on my truck's heated seat, and through a trainer's rubdown. There's no way I'll sit out a game with a *mattress*-related injury, so I ask the trainer to slap a lidocaine patch on it, then go out to the field.

Derek's running fielding drills with Travis and Angelides, who's practicing recovering balls out of the dirt and winging them to second base. For a while, I just watch. There's a harmony to the game that makes it peaceful, especially on a day like today, the stadium roof open but the weather otherwise cool.

Derek looks good at second base. Even among guys who are natural athletes, he's particularly willing to try stuff again and again until he gets it right.

Except...

But no, it's not fair to blame him for us not being together. It's a decision I made and he agreed with. A mature one. The right one, except it twinges the way my back does—a pang that's becoming increasingly impossible to ignore.

At the end of the day, we still play on the same team. We still need to work together, to be friends and teammates.

"Hey, Chason," Derek yells from the field, "you gonna come out here or are you gonna stand on the sidelines?" A cheerful ask, punctuated by the bright flash of his smile.

I gesture to my back, which feels better but not completely relaxed. "Just got worked on."

Derek's demeanor immediately goes from playful to clubhouse leader. He waves to Angelides, then comes over to me. "You okay?" Derek asks, looking a little overconcerned given that I only have a sore back.

"Just slept on it funny."

Travis cracks up from where he's standing on first base. "How do you get hurt sleeping?"

Derek's eyes narrow skeptically. "You sure?" he asks with such legitimate concern that my heart squeezes.

"For real," I say, reassuring him, "I got this mattress from some place online and it turns out I probably should have gone shopping at an actual store. There's a lump or something."

A totally normal ballpark conversation. Except that I know Derek's bed is ridiculously comfortable because I've slept in it. "You should get a better bed," he says.

Don't I know it.

He's about to say something more, but I keep going. "Don't worry. I'm working on it." And don't say that I'm also working on a lot of stuff.

Like how to get over him.

15

Derek

I can't stop thinking about Adam's bed as I get ready for our game that night.

Or my own for that matter.

How I haven't replaced the damaged one in my spare room, even though I need to. I've been researching mattresses in my spare time. Who knew there were so many options? There's organic, cotton, latex foam and on and on.

I never planned to devote so much attention to bedding, but I'm in the market too.

That's what I wanted to say when he cut me off.

But I can read between the lines. Adam

needs to concentrate on himself, his new home, his family, baseball.

It's all good. I'm doing the same.

Well, not family. But...friends and baseball, which both feel like family.

I channel my energy into focusing on the game for the rest of the evening, and it pays off—we win.

Which I love, but winning was a little more fun when I went home with Adam.

* * *

When I'm home later, rooting around the kitchen, there's a knock on the door. It can only be Travis. When I open it, the gregarious first baseman thrusts a couple of bottles of beer at me. "If I'm buying, you're cooking."

"Obviously," I say drily.

"That's how we do it," he says.

"It sure is," I say.

Because...I have a routine with Travis. This is my life. Hanging out with my teammate-slash-best friend after hours. Snacking, watching TV, talking sports.

Simple and mostly satisfying.

Quickly, I make sandwiches, then we settle on the couch with beers. Travis flips through my queue before arriving on a show where couples check out homes for sale. "Maybe not that one," I say, a phantom pain lodging in my chest as I take a drink.

Travis gives me an assessing look, then toggles to the next option. "If you say so."

We watch a crime drama, eating and drinking, commenting on possible suspects. Mostly I check my phone screen between bites, searching for—what else—mattresses.

Hmm. Do I want one that's good for a side sleeper? Wait. Nope. Adam sleeps on his side.

I groan quietly.

Maybe after I replace the mattress, I'll stop thinking about the guy so damn much.

"Anything good there?" Travis asks absently. "Your phone that is."

If anyone else asked, they might be busting me for checking out my screen. But this is Travis. This is our routine. "Just debating if I want to go vegan."

He whips his head from the TV. "What?"

I show him my phone. "I need to replace a mattress, and vegan mattresses are good for the environment," I grumble.

"You and Chason," he says with a laugh.

Yes, he knows I date guys, but does he know Adam and I had a thing? Not that I care, but what happened with Adam and me isn't my story alone to tell. It's *ours*. "What?" I ask sharply.

Travis shoots me a look like I'm clueless. "Chason was saying earlier he needed a bed too. His mattress is all jacked. The two of you are both looking for new beds. Oh, did you think I meant..."

I did. For a few seconds.

I sigh, annoyed with myself for being worried. But I'm annoyed because I want what I can't have.

Travis sighs too, but it's a thoughtful sound. "You know, Miller, if there's stuff going on, you can tell me, right?" And he says *stuff* like he knows what's up and is waiting for me to clarify it. "I'm cool with...anything."

I smile. I do appreciate that offer, but I'm not sure I want to serve up my insides. "I'm good. But thanks. That means a lot."

"Sure, man." Travis's tone is skeptical, then he adds, "I'm glad you're good, but it'd be okay if you weren't."

That's more emotional awareness than I'm expecting from *Travis*. "I'll be fine."

Another *uh huh*. "Sometimes it's unhealthy to push stuff down," he says.

Something other teammates have said before, as well as a few therapists. That there's no avoiding feelings even if you want to.

"So when I'm feeling like that," Travis continues, "I try to burp as loudly as I can. Really helps, you know, psychologically."

Which is more like it.

Travis has a point. Maybe I don't want to push stuff down anymore.

Maybe this life of eating sandwiches and watching TV I don't care about isn't enough.

Maybe hanging with a teammate in the evenings isn't the end game for me.

If I keep denying what I want, it'll come out eventually.

Right now, this second, I know what I want. I'm not sure I can have it. There's no guarantee.

But at the very least, I can try.

I pick up my phone. This time I don't look at mattresses. I draft a message to Adam.

Derek: Hey so, I need a mattress too. Want to go shopping together? As friends?

At the very least, I want to be friends with him. That's a place to start, and maybe then I can ask for what I want. Except...I want more. So much more. I delete the last line, erasing *As friends*. I'll take friendship, but first I'll swing for the fences.

I hit send.

A little while after Travis leaves, my phone pings. My heart jumps when I read the message.

Adam: I'd like that.

16

Adam

I check my reflection in the mirror. Nice short sleeve button-down. Clean-shaven jaw. Jeans that fit well.

My hair is a little messy. Or not messy enough, maybe?

Stop thinking about your hair. It's not a date.

Too bad my pulse is surging like it is a date. I run a hand through my hair, turn away from the mirror and take off. It's a Monday morning. Normally, I'd sleep in.

Instead, I'm wide awake and ridiculously excited to be heading to a mattress warehouse at the edge of the city.

When I arrive, I scan the parking lot for

Derek's truck, spotting it at the edge of the lot. He's here first, and my nerves spike, since I'll see him any second.

I should not be nervous to shop for a freaking mattress. *Not a date, not a date.* If I tell myself that enough, it might make it true.

As I head inside, I try to approach this like a game. I'm not nervous on the field. I know how to play. I anticipate, I react, I perform.

But those guidelines don't apply when I open the door to find Derek waiting inside.

My heart stutters. It's unfair how I react to him.

Somehow, he's even more handsome than the night of the rescue dog fundraiser. He wore a suit then. Now he's wearing shorts and a navy polo shirt that hugs his chest. And does funny things to mine.

Did he also dress like this is a date?

Don't go there.

"Hey Adam, did you make a list of all your mattress requirements?" he says in that dry amused tone.

Like that, my nerves vanish.

"As a matter of fact, I did," I say, striding over to him.

He claps my shoulder. A friendly gesture, but my breath catches.

"Let's see it," he says, standing next to me. So close, I can smell his cologne. That rainwater scent that transfers to his sheets. Right, I need to stop thinking about Derek in bed. Which would be easier if we weren't in a mattress store. I grab my phone, click on my notes, and show him the specs I detailed: degree of firmness, density of cushioning, and the number and gauge of coils. My ideal bed.

Well, my ideal bed, minus one element: Derek.

"What do you think?" I look at him, trying to school my expression so my face doesn't say *I miss you so much*.

His blue eyes sparkle. "I think that sounds like a perfect bed," he says, then he leads the way.

He weaves through the store, stopping in front of a king-size bed. He pushes his hand against it, testing the springs. "Too firm," he declares.

"Let me try." I press down too.

"What? You don't trust me?" he teases.

"Just wanted to try it for myself. Can't a guy test a mattress?"

A sly smile. "Sure. A guy can," he says, then heads to another mattress, waving me over.

I sit at the edge of this one, testing it. It's downright pillowy. "This one's pretty comfortable, I say, looking up at him.

"Comfy? Didn't see that on your list of requirements."

"It was implied," I say. "You know, the way your bed is."

"You liked my...bed?" he asks, voice pitching up with hope.

I liked his bed, yeah, but I liked what it represented. Being with him. I miss that so much I can feel the missing in my bones. I pat the mattress, suddenly feeling bolder than I expected. "I did like your bed," I say quietly.

"Good," he says firmly, like he's making a declaration. I hear what he doesn't say—*he liked me in it*. The way I liked being in it.

The mattress dips as Derek sits next to me, and I'm struck with how right this feels. Him, here. Us, together.

Not just on a bed. But on the couch. At home.

It all felt right. All those times we spent together felt right.

"It is comfortable," he says, but he frowns. "Maybe too comfortable. A good mattress needs to be a little firm to stand up to . . ." He turns a slight, un-Derek red.

"Well, so you can get some mileage out of it."

He pops back up and offers me a hand. That is so couple-y. And I love it. I lift my hand to take his, but he jerks his hand back right away. Like he realized his faux pas.

But I saw his intention.

Even when he clears his throat and weaves to another section of the store. As I watch him walk, I try to hold on to the reasons for resisting that felt vital a day ago.

He's my teammate.

I should focus on the game.

My life has changed radically in the past few months. All weighed against Derek offering me his hand in a mattress store. I want to take it.

Touching him, connecting with him—that's all that mattered in the moment. Maybe it'll stop mattering any second, but when he finds the next mattress, and flops down on it, my heart gallops.

I want *this*.

But it's not just the bed or the sex.

It's him.

All my reasons are good ones. Level-headed and thorough and *nice*. I flash back to the first night in Phoenix. To him kneeling on the floor. When he demanded I tell him what

I wanted. Even after a few hours of knowing me he could tell that I sometimes have trouble articulating that.

Derek's been clear from the start. I'm the guy with complications. My ex, my trade, my reasons. But are they really reasons...or am I just making excuses?

He's a teammate.

As if people don't sometimes date at the office, even if my office is a ballpark.

I should focus on work.

I've been playing better baseball since I got here, not in spite of Derek but because of him.

My life has just changed radically in the past few months.

So maybe I should change too.

Because this doesn't feel like two friends shopping for mattresses. I feel the same wild possibilities I felt when Derek and I looked at apartments together.

Tentatively, I sit down on the mattress. I turn to Derek, who's waiting for me. To make a decision. To take a chance.

"So, Adam, does this meet your needs?" he asks.

"It's a good mattress." I press my hand to its surface, watching the memory foam shape itself around my palm. "I'd like to get to know it better."

Amusement creases the corners of his eyes. "You'd like to get to know the...mattress better?"

I smile. "Feels like it's a mattress I could really rely on. That it'd be supportive of me when I need it. That it'd fit really well in my apartment or...wherever."

Derek's smile broadens.

"Also," I add, "I definitely want to take it to bed."

"Adam, are we still talking about a mattress?"

"You're going to make me say it?"

Derek pushes up on his elbows, his eyes sparking with hope and happiness. "I'm always going to make you say it."

"I want to wake up in your bed some mornings. I want to pick up coffee for you on other mornings. I want to go to the ballpark with you. Some nights, I want you to come over. Other nights I want to go home with you. I just want you," I say. "I know there's stuff to figure out, but we'll figure it out."

He sits up, grabs my face, and pulls me in for a kiss, something more passionate than is appropriate for a mattress store on a weekday morning. I don't care.

Eventually, we pull apart. "So, is this one a keeper?" Derek asks.

I nod, frantically, then go talk with the salesperson as fast as humanly possible to arrange for this mattress to be delivered.

"Should arrive sometime later today," I tell Derek when I'm done.

"Maybe we should go back to your place and wait for it," Derek says. "Make sure it arrives and everything."

"How responsible of you," I say, drily, even if my heart is beating against my chest. Even if I want to drag him back against that mattress and to hell with everything else.

It must show, because he runs a finger over my hand, a quick gesture that does nothing to settle my pulse. "Invite me over," he says. "I think you owe me a tour."

We go to my apartment and I show him my place for the first time.

Correction: We barely make it to the couch, tumbling into each other, kissing and touching and stripping.

And coming together.

Then, we go to the ballpark.

Together.

EPILOGUE

Adam

October in Seattle is strangely hot. But maybe that's just the sweat I'm working up hauling my things from my truck in the parking garage, up the elevator, and down the hall.

Into Derek's condo.

Only now, it's *our* condo.

I carry a box inside, setting it next to the bed in our bedroom. "That should be everything."

Derek's here, looking exactly like I saw him five minutes ago and also, perfect. I lean over, kissing him, then pull back.

"What do you think?" I ask, looking around.

"Took you long enough," he deadpans.

"Ha. Yes, the last few months when I lived two blocks away were torture," I say, since I was here nearly every night when we were in town.

"Exactly. Now you're where you belong," he says. A statement. The truth, pure and simple.

"I am," I say.

Seconds later, there's a knock on the front door. A loud "Miller!" follows.

Derek raises a brow playfully. I do the same. I'm sure we're both thinking the same thing. If Travis hasn't figured us out yet, he's about to now.

"Did you want to say something to him about us?" I ask as we leave the bedroom.

Us. A relationship that lasted the rest of the season, through Seattle almost, but not quite, making it to the playoffs. Still, a better outcome than I could have ever hoped for in St. Louis, in more ways than one.

We haven't *announced* we're together since we wanted to just *be together* first. But we've been planning to tell our teammates soon. I didn't think it'd be today, but life has a way of surprising you.

I'm ready. "We can start with Travis," I add.

A flash of guilt passes in Derek's eyes. "He might already know. He said something to me a couple months ago—the day I asked you to go mattress shopping with me." My surprise must show because Derek adds, "He's actually emotionally perceptive."

"You're right," I manage. "That is kind of shocking...Or maybe not, truth be told."

Travis has been...astute, and aware. He encouraged Derek to let me stay with him right away. He knew Derek was the kind of guy who'd open his home to a teammate. Travis knows he too can come over any night and hang with us.

We stop in the living room, a few feet from the door. Derek taps me on the arm. "Want to tell him?" With that, nerves, the edge of his chewed lip. A reminder that the team is his family.

"Miller!" Travis yells again. "Whatever you're doing, I've seen it all before."

I take one of his hands in mine. This is important. "I'm good to tell him if you are."

Derek nods, apprehensive, and I have to kiss him, and so I do, a kiss followed by another knock. "He's my closest friend," Derek says, semi-apologetically.

"He's your closest friend," I say with a smile, "so we should tell him."

"He'll be cool with it," Derek says.

"You remember when you told him how to pronounce my name and he did it, no question?"

Derek nods.

"He looks up to you."

Derek's eyebrows rise. "Really?"

"Yeah, really. Clubhouse leader and all that." I give his hand a squeeze. "So we can tell him if you want."

With that decided, Derek pulls the door open. "Hey," Derek says. "We want to—"

Travis smirks. "—Tell me what? That you're boning or whatever?"

Derek lets out a long, slow breath, but he doesn't drop my hand. "Yeah, pretty much."

"I already knew that," Travis says, with a satisfied shrug. "Maybe before you did." He taps a finger against his temple. "Now who's the clubhouse leader?"

"Definitely not you," Derek says, laughing.

"Yeah, probably not." Travis drums a hand against his jeans. "You cooking or what? I'm starving."

"Sure," Derek says. "Want to stay for lunch?"

"I thought you'd never ask," he says, then he winks. "But don't worry. I'll take off after and you can enjoy being...*roomies* again."

I laugh. "We will."

"We definitely will," Derek echoes.

And we do for the rest of the off-season. We spent most of it together, here in Seattle, going out to the trendy restaurants in our neighborhood, checking out endless coffee shops, playing golf.

And seeing my family. He comes with me to Houston to meet my parents. He's the perfect gentleman at dinner, but later, when we're alone walking through downtown, he confesses he was nervous the whole time.

"I just wanted them to like me," he says.

I stop on the street, smile, catch his lips in a kiss. "They do. Just like I do," I say. But that's not true. "Actually, I love you."

His gaze turns tender. "I love you too, Adam."

* * *

In February, Arizona is already sweltering as we get ready for the fundraiser together—in our rental for spring training.

The house is a single story with stucco walls and a red tiled roof. It looks just like every other house around it. Except this one has both our signatures on the lease for the next few months.

Derek shoots me a dirty look while I button my shirt, his voice rumbling. "You in a suit..."

"You sure liked it last year," I say.

"I like it this year too," he says, then stalks over to me, and plants a possessive kiss to my lips.

I shiver. "Will you do that at the fundraiser too?"

He smiles. "I will."

"I'm looking forward to that. And to playing craps again. I watched some tutorials. I think I've got the hang of it now," I say as we head to the door, then I stop, something nagging at my memory from the night a year ago. "Hey, why was five your lucky number?"

Derek wiggles a brow. "Oh, that?"

"Yeah, that?" I prod, more curious now. "What was that all about?"

"That was just the number of orgasms I wanted to give you that night."

I laugh. "Ambitious."

He squeezes my ass. "Was I, Chason? I'm well past five now."

Hundreds, I'd say. "Let's get going then. You can work on another five after the fundraiser," I say.

Then, Derek hauls me in for a kiss, his lips against mine as we embrace in the promising Arizona sunset.

THE END

Want to be the first to learn of sales, new releases, preorders and special freebies from Lauren Blakely and KD Casey? Sign up for this exclusive MM VIP mailing list here! Don't miss the first standalone in our Dirty Players series! Dirty Slide is a rivals-to-lovers baseball romance!

Interested in Alex's story? Be sure to check out KD Casey's DIAMOND RING, coming April 2023.

Estranged former teammates reunite for one last run at a championship, fanning old resentments—and old sparks between them.

And if you were intrigued by Maddox, his romance is told in Lauren Blakely's TURN

ME ON a sexy, emotional, epic romance you won't want to miss!

And check out FIRE SEASON, KD's latest friends-to-lovers baseball romance, available now!

Charlie Braxton has it all: a wicked curveball, a beautiful wife, and the kind of money and attention that's attached to a professional baseball contract. Except his famous curveball comes with intense social anxiety, his wife is actually his soon-to-be ex-wife, and the money... Well, suffice it to say, he knows what it's like to be treated like an ATM. But at least he's better off than the new guy.

Relief pitcher Reid Giordano is struggling to maintain his sobriety—and his roster spot. The press, along with a heck of a lot of his new Oakland teammates, seem to think his best baseball days are behind him. Only Charlie Braxton gives him the benefit of the doubt—and a place to stay when Reid finds himself short on cash...and friends.

When their growing friendship turns into an unexpected attraction, and that ignites a romance, both Charlie and Reid must grapple with what it means to be more than teammates. And as their season winds down, they'll need to walk away...or go out there and give it everything they've got.

Here's s sneak preview of **Fire Season,** available everywhere!

Charlie

This has the feeling of a date, especially when they get there and the hostess informs them it'll be a few minutes before they can get seated. They wait at the bar. Charlie orders a beer and a seltzer with lime without thinking and hands it to Reid, who's looking around at the other diners, couples in low conversation over flickering electric candles. "I thought we were supposed to get you out and meeting people."

Though he doesn't sound disappointed, especially when the waiter seats them, then pauses, taking in Charlie's height. "Yeah, it's really him," Reid says.

And Charlie resists the urge to tap his foot against his under the table.

The waiter returns with a wine list, bottles priced expensively even for a San Francisco restaurant, and looks a little pinched when Charlie says they're all set for drinks, as if seeing the size of his tip diminish.

They're left alone after that. Reid doesn't actually get a steak, instead ordering short ribs and greens, asking them to leave off the Parmesan if possible. Charlie is about to order pork chops before he stops himself. "Is that a problem?"

Because he did some googling about keeping kosher when Reid mentioned he preferred beef bacon. A search that yielded a set of dietary restrictions that seemed confusing even for someone who plays a sport with the infield fly rule.

"I keep kosher the way I don't drink," Reid says. "It's for me. Eat whatever you want." Punctuated with a shrug, like maybe Charlie's said the wrong thing and he's letting it go.

"I didn't mean to..." Charlie begins, and the problem with not having his words filled in for him is now he has to find the correct ones. "I'm just not used to being around, uh, religious people."

Reid tilts his head. "You think guys who have Romans 1-2-3-4 or whatever in their Twitter bios ain't religious?"

That's different. Though it's kind of hard to say why. Something Charlie never really thought to examine before. He shifts. His chair complains at his size. "I just want to get stuff right." Honest, maybe too honest, though Reid flashes a look at him, a pleased glance from under his eyelashes that'd be a date kind of look. If this was a date.

"You did. Wanting to get it right is like ninety percent of it."

"What's the other ten percent?"

Reid nudges his chair closer. Their feet brush momentarily. He smiles again. "I'll be sure to let you know when I find out."

They get a few appetizers to split, Reid talking about how he doesn't understand fancy-ass Italian food or tiny servings while enthusiastically eating his fill of them. Whatever stuff he needed to unload about the game, he already did with his therapist—and to Elbow Patches, who asked about his pitch arsenal and frowned at Reid's succinct response.

"What're you gonna do with Avis when we're on the road?" he asks.

"Christine says she'll take her. She's an artist, so she's home all the time."

"An artist?"

"Yeah, mostly pottery, though she does stuff with textiles. Here—" Charlie pulls out his phone, opening up Christine's Instagram to a picture of her next to a piece that's in progress, her hair pulled back from her face, tattoos visible around her shoulders and arms.

Reid looks between the phone and Charlie and back like there's been some mistake. "That's not really..." He looks embarrassed.

"Not what you were expecting?"

"Just recalibrating what your type is. 'Cause I gotta say, I was expecting more Texas beauty queen and less California artist."

"Believe me, so was my mom," Charlie says, and Reid laughs loudly at that. "She came around to Christine when she realized 'artist' didn't mean she was flaky, though she's got some things to say about the divorce. She would have preferred a nice church-going girl. Someone who wanted kids."

"Christine doesn't?"

Charlie shakes his head. "But then I don't feel one way or another about kids, and that's a whole other thing. Avis is kid enough for now."

"Oh, here." Reid takes out his phone. On it, a set of pictures: Avis in her crate, a line of drool dripping down onto her blanket.

"How many pictures you got of her?"

Charlie pauses before he scrolls through Reid's photo roll.

"You can take a look."

Most are of Reid and guys Charlie doesn't recognize, a few plates of barbecue from what looks like Omaha. No close-up pictures with Reid's face pressed against someone else's, something Charlie is relieved at even if he has no real right to be. There's a recurring picture, snapshots of Reid's semicolon tattoo, enough times in his photo roll with different lighting that he must just take them periodically.

It's visible now, his arm upturned on the table, the sleeve of his Henley pushed to the elbows, the blue-and-white bracelet circling his wrist. Close enough for Charlie to hold his hand or rub his thumb over the semicolon tattoo and ask him why he takes so many pictures of it. If those pictures are for good days or bad days or just because he's bored, because baseball is often boring when it's not awful or ecstatic.

He lays his hand next to Reid's, a little humming film of air between them. Reid looks down, expression curious, before shifting to take another long swallow of water.

Charlie does the same, wondering what it

might be like not just to sleep with Reid, but to *be* with him. If this not-quite-a-date was something real. A pull he hasn't felt since he met Christine at a bar, with a cluster of her girlfriends, and let her demand his phone so she could add her number. Something in the comparison doesn't sit easy with him, so he takes a sip of his beer and asks Reid to text him a picture of Avis that's usable for social media.

Their food comes, and they set about the business of eating, Reid talking about other ribs he's eaten—most from before he "went kosher"—and the best places to get barbecue on the minor-league circuit. About a rib-eating contest he foolishly entered against a little guy in an obscure outpost in rural Kansas, only to get his ass kicked by someone who could *eat*.

"I'm telling you, I should've brought the guy home," Reid says. "My grandma likes anyone who can eat like that." He takes a last bite of his short ribs, practically scraping the plate. "She'd like you plenty."

Charlie's end of the table is occupied by his emptied plate and the few appetizer dishes the waitstaff haven't collected. "Yeah?"

"Nice church-going Texas boy who eats her cooking. What's not to like?"

"I mostly don't go anymore. To church, I mean. My parents do, but it's not something I looked for out here." Something Christine and he decided early in their relationship. Another thing his mom frowned over, like he wasn't fifty percent of that decision. "Your grandma wouldn't mind you bringing someone home who isn't Jewish, um, generally speaking?"

Reid gives him a slow smile. "Generally speaking? Letitia—my ex—is French Catholic from Vermont. And it's just my dad's mom who's Jewish. I got converted when I was a baby kinda 'just in case.'" And he does air quotes, a thick Jersey accent with it, in what must be an imitation of one of his parents. "It's from your mom's side, usually. Well, depends—the whole religion's kind of 'answers will vary'—so my folks wanted to be sure."

And Charlie thought of being Jewish as something you were or you weren't. He feels around for a question and hopes it's the right one. "Is that typical?"

Reid inclines his head to one side. "Not really."

"Sorry if that was rude—I really don't know anything about this."

"It's all good." With it, a hand on the

tabletop in reassurance, glancing contact with Charlie's own. "Generally, don't ask if people converted, if that's what you're getting at. It can get complicated. My mom actually tried to baptize me too, but the rabbi said they had to pick one, so here I am."

"I, uh, figured with the tattoo." And Charlie's face goes uncomfortably warm at having mentioned the tattoo that stretches from Reid's side to his hip, a set of praying hands and a Bible verse.

Reid laughs, quieter than his usual laugh. His eyes crease at the corners. He looks relaxed, handsome, and fond, and Charlie somehow woke up thinking he was, if not straight, at least straight-adjacent: an increasingly distant continent from whatever he is now.

"That one might have been 'cause I lost a bet," Reid says. "I don't really remember." He rolls his water glass in his hands. "We were never really that observant—you know, menorah with the Christmas tree kind of family. When I first got sober, I kinda liked that there are so many holidays and rules. There's always something to look forward to. I can't really explain it. It just feels right. Like it'd been waiting for me to come back to it in my own time."

He shrugs, smiling, like he's embarrassed at having said all that. And Charlie can't grasp his hand in a restaurant, can't reach across and say, *I think I know how that is.* "I'm probably boring you anyway," Reid adds.

"It's, um, cool." Which feels woefully inadequate. "I mean, I like hearing you talk about it."

A statement about as transparent as Reid's water glass, and Reid gives him a different kind of smile, warm, that makes Charlie want to say screw it and kiss him.

Their waiter interrupts, clearing dishes, handing them dessert menus.

"You want anything?" Charlie asks.

It really does feel like a date, the two of them considering a list of possibilities. The only things left on their table are Charlie's beer glass, netted with foam, and Reid's half-full water. The restaurant is quiet, an instrumental song Charlie doesn't recognize, the polite murmurs of other eaters.

Reid discards the menu on the table, its edge in the puddle left by his water glass. "I'm pretty full. I got another idea. If you're up for it."

A hundred possibilities, provided in flashed suggestion. "Of course."

"I haven't asked you yet."

"Whatever it is, I'm sure I'm good with it."

And his answering smile makes Charlie's heart beat anticipatorily against his ribs.

If you enjoyed this sneak preview, be sure to check out FIRE SEASON!

Want to know more about **TURN ME ON**? Here's a sneak peek!

Maddox...

The second they're out of earshot, I turn to Zane, and don't mince words. "I owe you an apology. I didn't say who I was at the bar because I was having too much fun talking to you, and I'm sorry. I truly hope I didn't fuck things up for us when it comes to business. I would love to work with you, and you have my word I don't make it a practice to hit on clients. That was a first for me."

The man remains entirely impassive, turning his glass of water round and round. Then he stops fiddling and tilts his head to meet my eyes.

I still can't read what's behind his gorgeous greens, and it's driving me crazy.

"First time you hit on a client, you say?"

I swallow roughly. "Yes."

"And what made me your first, Maddox?" The way he says my name sounds like sex and heat.

Maybe that's a sign I'm forgiven. "Do you really want me to go there?"

His stoic expression doesn't shift, but his eyes darken with bedroom intensity. "Yes. Go there, Maddox."

He's giving me a goddamn command? Gritting my teeth, I resist the shudder that whooshes down my chest. But it *is* an order, delivered quietly and clearly, and I obey. "You're just..." I pause, collecting my thoughts, before I speak the truth. "Kind of irresistible."

You can find TURN ME ON everywhere at a discount right now!

ALSO BY

Be sure to try all of Lauren's USA Today Bestselling MM romances!

Men of Summer Series

One Time Only

A Guy Walks Into My Bar

The Bromance Zone

Hopelessly Bromantic Duet

She also writes many MF romances including...

FULL PACKAGE, the #1 New York Times Bestselling romantic comedy!

BIG ROCK, the hit New York Times Bestselling standalone romantic comedy!

You'll love KD Casey's MM baseball romances!

UNWRITTEN RULES, an emotional second-chance baseball romance debut!

FIRE SEASON, an emotional "they were roommates!" friends-to-lovers romance.

DIAMOND RING, a sexy, friends-to-enemies-to-lovers baseball romance.

ONE TRUE OUTCOME, a sexy, veteran/rookie romance!

CONTACT

You can find Lauren on Twitter at LaurenBlakely3, Instagram at LaurenBlakelyBooks, Facebook at LaurenBlakelyBooks, or online at LaurenBlakely.com. You can also email her at laurenblakelybooks@gmail.com

KD Casey would love to hear from you! Find KD on Twitter, Instagram, and Facebook at KDCaseyWrites, online at kdcaseywrites.com, or email at kdcaseywrites@gmail.com.

Printed in Great Britain
by Amazon